HOSTAGES OF FATE

On a remote Scottish island, Cressida Bellingham seeks peace and solitude. Instead, she finds adventure and danger when she meets Jon Grant, a man convinced the key to his financial ruin lies in Quoyne House where Cressida is staying. Cressida and Jon are strongly attracted, but prejudice and suspicion threaten their relationship. Eerie happenings on the island intensify the mystery, and only if this is resolved can they face their personal dilemmas and find happiness together.

Books by Joyce Johnson
in the Linford Romance Library:

ROUGH MAGIC
BITTER INHERITANCE

JOYCE JOHNSON

HOSTAGES OF FATE

Complete and Unabridged

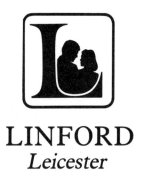

LINFORD
Leicester

First published in Great Britain in 1994

First Linford Edition
published 2000

British Library CIP Data

Johnson, Joyce, *1931 –*
    Hostages of fate.—Large print ed.—
Linford romance library
1. Love stories
2. Large type books
I. Title
813.5'4 [F]

ISBN 0–7089–5650–5

Published by
F. A. Thorpe (Publishing) Ltd.
Anstey, Leicestershire
Set by Words & Graphics Ltd.
Anstey, Leicestershire
Printed and bound in Great Britain by
T. J. International Ltd., Padstow, Cornwall

This book is printed on acid-free paper

1

'Montague!' Cressy's yell was torn from her and tossed into the howling blackness. 'Food — dinner,' she shrieked, with little hope. Out there in the darkness, Montague had found something much more interesting than anything Quoyne House could offer. If the wretched puppy didn't come in soon, it looked like a full-scale night hunt, with flashlight and wellies.

Tentatively, she stepped away from the shelter of the stone porch, and gasped as the banshee wind snatched at a swathe of thick, chestnut hair and whipped it, like a bandage, across her face. Even after living a month at Quoyne House, the total pitch-black night was still a shock, and her hair over her eyes didn't help matters.

Cressida Bellingham was a city girl. For her, the night sky had always been a dark bowl, upturned over city lights. Here, apart from the last faded glimmer of twilight away on the horizon, there wasn't a light to be seen on the Scottish isle of Pentsay.

'Monty.' She tried, without success, to inject a wheedling note into her voice, wondering why on earth her godfather had chosen such an undoglike name for the puppy he'd insisted on giving her, in spite of her objections.

'Company,' he'd said firmly. 'If you won't have the Murrays living in, you'll have Montague. Otherwise, the deal's off.'

She'd given in gracefully, but Montague was a liability she could have done without.

Shivering, she thought longingly of the cosy library inside, tea-table drawn up to the log fire, crumpets at the ready under the grill, kettle beginning to purr.

Tea and crumpets! A symbol of how her life had narrowed. Last year, at this time, even a snatched lunch-break would have seemed a luxury. Now, tea and crumpets were the highlight of the entire day!

She stepped forward on to the gravelled driveway and jumped as the yellow square of light shining from the hall disappeared, and the door crashed to behind her. To her horror, she realised, that the latch was down — she was locked out, presumably, along with Montague, the only other living soul for miles around.

Fifteen minutes later, she was still outside. Every window was double-locked, and double-glazed. Her wealthy godfather, Sir Ian Mackay, might be a touch eccentric, but he was a firm believer in his creature comforts — and tight security. Even though Pentsay's crime rate was probably zero, he obviously didn't believe in taking chances, Cressy thought, as she put down the crowbar she'd been using, trying to pry open a downstairs window.

She stood irresolute, getting colder by

the minute. A spatter of icy rain struck her cheeks, and she winced. Problem solving had been her life in London, now she was to be beaten by a small thing like a Yale lock and no key. At least in London there'd be telephone directories, locksmiths and the police. On Pentsay, there was nothing, except a few people — herself, some fishermen, the Murrays, sheep, and the high-spirited Montague.

Flora and Ben Murray came daily to Quoyne House, ostensibly to caretake, although in reality, Cressy suspected, they had instructions from her god-father to take care of her! They had keys, but had left earlier in the day to visit family on the mainland.

There was nothing for it — it had to be a break-in. She'd freeze to death if she stayed out much longer. Also, normally without fear, Cressy had to admit that it was getting spooky. Inside, the house looked friendly — the lights were on, but its gaunt façade, and the surrounding dark hills, pressed in as bleak, unfriendly shapes, and the moaning wind tore at spikey, winter trees.

In a bright, sunny, sitting-room, it was easy enough to dismiss Flora Murray's tales and legends of the lochs and hills as superstitious nonsense. Now, with a backward glance towards the distant, dark waters, she could easily imagine monsters rising from the deep or, nearer still, the grey man of the moor, said to haunt the solitary traveller. Cressy shivered — even the disobedient Montague would be welcome at this moment.

Picking up the crowbar again, she weighted it in her hand. The small cloakroom window would have to go. Ben Murray could easily replace it in the morning. She drew back her arm and heard a harsh sound behind her. Simultaneously, her hand was wrenched down, and she was pinned firmly by an arm across her windpipe.

A deep voice, laced with anger, ground into her ear. 'What do you think you're doing?'

Cressy couldn't stop the scream gasping up from her throat. She dropped the crowbar and tried to turn, but the hands held her, increasing the pressure, like a vice.

The voice rasped, 'Burglars get short shrift in Pentsay — we don't usually bother the police!' The tone was deadly, icily serious.

Panic knotted Cressy's stomach. As she tried to shake the hold, her long hair tumbled free.

'Ah!' The grip loosened slightly, the voice changed, but was no less icy. 'A woman! You must be the girl who — '

The pressure on her throat eased. 'Let me go. You're hurting me,' Cressy shouted, struggling to free herself but, never for a moment forgetting to keep her head lowered and her hair around her face.

'Get away,' she gritted, her free arm flailing in order to strike any part she could find. Her left hand struck a solid blow into a hard, male stomach. She twisted and, in the darkness, could make out long legs; felt the waxy texture of a Barbour coat, and knew this was no spirit of the hills. It was all solid, angry man, whose other hand caught her wildly threshing arm and forced her round to face him.

'I can't see you — what . . . ?'

Desperately, Cressy arched back. He mustn't see her face, but he was dragging her over to the yellow square of light, cut by the uncurtained window. 'No! No — don't — how dare — ' Fear of that yellow square gave her increased strength as she lashed out with her foot, feeling a satisfying crack as a lucky aim hit his shin. She was glad she had her boots on!

He gasped with pain and slackened his grip on one of her hands.

Swinging her free fist upwards with all her strength, she heard the crack repeated, her bare knuckles making contact with solid bone. Cressy was tall, but he was a taller man and, in a quick reflex, had ducked his head to one side, avoiding the full impact of her blow, but he was caught off balance and swayed away from her.

She pulled free, and darted back into the dark porch, crouching behind one of the stone columns. There were no lights, but she pulled the wide cowl of her sweater up round her ears. She was no longer cold. Fear and adrenalin furnaced round her blood as she waited in the darkness to see what the man would do next.

Her heart thumped painfully, and she tried to bring her breathing back to normal. She wished she hadn't dropped the crowbar! The only potential weapon was an iron boot-scraper by the front door, which should stop whoever he was in his tracks, if he attempted to grab her again. It was very heavy, but in her four weeks on Pentsay, she'd begun to regain her fitness. Clasping it to her chest, she waited, tense, straining to see into the darkness.

She heard movement before she saw

the dark, looming shadow almost on top of her, with one foot on the porch step. He looked totally menacing, and Cressy held out the iron door-stop in front of her. 'Don't you dare come a step nearer.' She was pleased to hear that her voice was strong and even. 'I wouldn't like to drop this — accidentally — on your foot. It's pretty lethal. I've warned you — it'd be self defence,' she added desperately, as he took another step towards her.

'Who'd believe you, here on Pentsay?' Contempt curled in his voice, which was educated English, with only a trace of Highland music, and jaggedly discordant in anger. 'You wild cat. What are you up to?'

'I can ask you the same — and keep your distance!' She tried to raise the iron weapon, but it was heavy and the effort made her gasp.

'Put that down, before you drop it on your own foot. What were you going to do with this crowbar?'

Cressy was alarmed to see that he

had picked it up and was swinging it easily by his side. Her grasp on the old door-scraper was numbing her wrists, but she gritted her teeth and held on. After the pain she'd endured recently, it was nothing!

'This is my property,' she flung at him, 'and if I want to take a crack at an intruder, that's too bad for you.'

'Just as well for you, you didn't,' his voice grated out of the darkness. 'My type of chivalry doesn't extend to turning the other cheek. An eye for an eye is my philosophy, and I wouldn't give much for your chances in a straight fight. As far as I'm concerned, you're a burglar breaking into a neighbour's property.'

'Neighbour? This is — '

'I know who Quoyne House belongs to. It is owned by Sir Ian Mackay, and he's not in residence at the moment. He's taken pity on some neurotic actress from London, and let his property to her. Someone who wants to hide away from the world. I presume that's who you are?'

The sneer was unmistakeable, and Cressy gasped. What an unbearable brute the man was. She'd never asked for pity — she did need this hideaway, but not in the way this hateful stranger was implying. But, if he knew her godfather, at least that implied a sort of respectability. He moved back, and she put the door-stop down, flexing her fingers against the returning blood rush.

'Well,' he asked curtly, 'you still haven't explained yourself. Why were you trying to break into the house?' He'd moved into the yellow square which Cressy had fought to avoid, and its light showed a craggy face, moulded in strong, dark planes. His eyes were hooded and hair overlong and curling, blowing in the wind. For all the well-modulated and civilised music of his voice, Cressy sensed he was comfortable and at one with the dark, stormy night. A wild primitive.

She shivered, keeping well away from

him. 'I'm not breaking in. The door slammed. I'm locked out, and I've lost Montague.' How feeble it sounded, she thought in annoyance. resenting his harsh bark of laughter.

'Locked out! And who's Montague — your boyfriend?'

The searing distaste in his voice roused her to fury. 'Yes — and no. Montague is a dog, not that it's any of your business. If you can't help, would you please take yourself off my — my godfather's premises.' In the darkness, she drew herself up to her full height.

The man thrust his hands into his pockets. 'And how do you propose to get back in?' he drawled. 'That is, after you've convinced me you've a right to be inside. For all I know, you have an accomplice lurking in the grounds, waiting until I've gone, to steal Sir Ian's family silver. Have you any identification on you?'

'Don't be so ridiculous.' Cressy bit her lip. 'I don't usually carry my passport or driving licence with me when I want to call in the dog! Sir Ian Mackay is my godfather, and he's loaned me Quoyne House for as long as I want it, though I can't see what it's got to do with you.'

'No — someone like you. I don't suppose you could.'

The frosty dislike in his voice stunned her. What did he mean — someone like her?

'Don't you have a spare key?' His question was curt.

'Of course I don't. Do you think I'm enjoying this freezing night air, being patronised by you? If I had a spare key, I'd be inside.'

'The Murray's will have a key. They're only five miles down the track. I don't suppose you're prepared to walk, but there's the Land-Rover in the stables.'

For a stranger, he seemed to know a lot about Quoyne House.

'You know the Murrays?'

'Of course. Everyone knows everyone on Pentsay. It's neighbourly, not like your neck of the woods — London!'

He sounded bitterly dismissive, and Cressy's hackles rose. She loved London. She'd known no other life and had revelled in its pacey, bustly glitter.

'If you're an example of local neighbourliness, I'm not impressed. The Murrays are away on the mainland. Otherwise I'd have no objection to walking to their house — the Land-Rover keys being inside the house.'

Sarcasm gave a sharp edge to her reply. She hated having to explain anything to the objectionable stranger, but he appeared to be her only hope, much as she hated his patronising contempt. There was something about him which told her he could get her back inside — if he wanted to. Although, at the moment, he seemed to be taking a perverse pleasure in keeping her outside in the wild, black night. Power showed in the strength of his dark shape.

He came back to the porch. She was glad she hadn't switched on the outside light before trying to call in the dog! Shrinking down even further into the cowl neck of her sweater, she shook her long hair around her face in a gesture which was becoming more habitual than she knew.

The man peered at her curiously, then leaned casually back against the wall. 'You could always spend the night at the pub. It's only six miles away. I'll walk you there if you like, I'm going that way.'

'Thanks very much,' she said coldly, 'but I'd prefer to break a window and spend the night there.'

'Pentsay Arms not good enough for you? London wine bars more your scene?'

Cressy clutched her arms across her chest, and closed her eyes. He was infuriating. 'Mind your own business, and don't let me keep you.' Her caustic tone matched his. 'Either go away, or help me get inside the house, if you can. I don't particularly care which.'

Unexpectedly, he put his hand out in

the darkness, and grasped her shoulder, drawing her towards him. 'Why are you cowering away? Let me see you.'

Her reaction was instant. With a yelp, she shook off his hand and ran away from him along the front of the house. 'Go!' she shouted, 'I can manage. Go away!'

A black shape came bounding out of the darkness, leaping up at her. Hysterical barking drowned out the wind's moans, as Montague finally arrived home for supper.

'Get down, you silly dog!' Cressy fended him off, but his delight at seeing his new mistress again sent him scurrying around in increasingly demented circles.

The tall man stepped forward into the square of light again, nearer to its beam now, and Cressy saw his face more clearly. It was craggy, with a wide, sensual mouth, deep-set eyes and a strong, square jawline. With a shock, she realised it was a familiar face, resembling one she ought to know, evoking a not too distant memory she couldn't quite place.

When the nightmare of the yapping Montague, the invincible Quoyne House, and the infuriating man had receded, her brain would no doubt function normally, and she'd remember. It could only be a resemblance, for it was unlikely there'd be anyone on Pentsay she knew.

She struggled with the dog, trying to grab his collar, but he wriggled and twisted, jumping up to lick her face. Suddenly, a warm hand touched hers over the collar, and a firm voice commanded. 'Down — at once!'

Instantly, as though shot, the puppy dropped motionless to the ground, and Cressy could sense him looking up at the dominant man. Her own hand still felt the warm imprint of the stranger's grasp.

'You're frozen,' he accused, in much the same tone as he'd commanded the dog to obedience. He handed her his jacket.

She backed away. 'No — I don't want it — '

'Put it on, I don't need it. I'm not a hot-house, city plant.'

Her protest was lost in the wind, as he strode purposely off round the back of the house. Resentful, but conscious of the blissful warmth of his coat, she called after him. 'I've tried all the doors and windows. There's no way in.' She noted the treacherous Montague, sidling after the broad figure, then she was alone in the darkness once more.

Trying to follow, she stumbled once or twice, and gave up. The grounds of Quoyne House were unfamiliar in the dark and, uneasily, she thought how well the stranger seemed to know his way around. A thought struck her — could her godfather have possibly appointed a second caretaker?

The voice which cut across her half-formed suspicion was grim and cold. 'You'll have no worries about burglars — Quoyne House is impregnable. Luckily for you, I've found a key.'

Cressy gasped. 'Where?' but he'd already put it in the lock. Panic engulfed her — the hall lights were blazing. In a minute he'd see her. As he turned the lock and started to open the door, she pushed past, reached around, snapped back the yale catch, and stood with her back to the closed front door. 'Thanks.' Her breathing was ragged. 'I'll be fine now. Here's your coat. Good-night.'

His stiff disapproval was palpable, even in the darkness. 'Normally, it would be customary to show basic hospitality.'

Cressy's flush was part fury, part embarrassment. Her circumstances weren't normal. 'Normally,' she ground out, 'visitors wouldn't be so patronisingly rude. Thank you again for unlocking my front door. I can't imagine we'd have anything to say to each other, even if I were to ask you in, which I'm not,' she ended hastily.

'Don't worry, I've no time for social chit-chat, and no sympathy with — '

he broke off abruptly before adding, 'Island manners dictate I finish the job you foisted on me, and see you safely inside.' His voice was as chill as the deep loch a mile beyond the house where Cressy had walked that morning. She'd dipped her fingers into the black waters — they were numb in a second. She felt the same numbness as the stranger loomed before her on the portico of Quoyne House.

Angrily, she eased the door back just sufficiently for her slender body to slide through. 'So — I'm in. You can go now,' she shot back at him, and slammed the door.

2

Leaning heavily against the door, Cressy breathed deeply to still her racing heart. What a dreadful man! What if her suspicion was true! She'd have to phone Sir Ian now. He'd kept his promise not to contact her until she was settled in, but she knew he'd be anxious, and the time felt right now. But — hot tea and buttered crumpets first, she promised, as the centrally heated warmth of the house flowed around her in welcoming waves.

Thawing out rapidly, she crossed the square, baronial hall, hung everywhere with rich plaids and tartans. The decor in Quoyne House made a definite statement about her godfather's Scottish ancestry. She'd never understood his determined nationalism until coming to Pentsay.

The loud jangle of the doorbell was

aggressive, not a polite announcement of arrival. She knew who it was, and why he was ringing. Montague — she'd forgotten all about him! She opened the door a fraction, and the puppy shot in, paws frantically scrabbling on the polished oak.

'You don't seem to care much for your animal's welfare — too wrapped up in self pity! You'd better learn to control him. There are a lot of sheep about and dogs that worry them don't last long here. Good-night!'

Cressy bent down and held on to Montague's collar as she listened to the receding scrunch of boots on the gravel path. What wouldn't she have given to have flung wide the door and hurled back a biting reply? Instead, she counted slowly to ten, released the dog, and went into the kitchen, concentrating her thoughts on hot tea.

Sir Ian had spared no expense on the kitchen. High tech to a bewildering degree, it had far more gadgets than Cressy would ever need for her sole occupancy. She knew her godfather entertained lavishly in the autumn and summer, flying in his guests himself on his own plane from Aberdeen to Kirkwall. Her parents had visited often, but somehow Cressy and her sister, Imogen, had missed out. Too busy, she thought ruefully, racketing round the world, looking for fame and fortune — Imogen chasing film or stage parts, Cressy, herself, following up news stories.

As always, a second before the phone rang, she knew Imogen was about to contact her. She picked up the receiver in the kitchen.

'That was quick.' Her twin's breathy, theatrical voice floated down the line.

'I'm right by the phone. I was thinking of you.'

'I haven't stopped thinking of you — ever since you left London to bury yourself on that remote island. How are you?'

'I'm fine. Stop worrying. I'm not an invalid. This is my choice, remember.

How's the play going?' Usually, that question brought a flood of theatre gossip and anecdotes, but not this time. Imogen was not to be side-tracked.

'It's OK. The understudies are having a run — so, I'm coming up to see you. I can fly up on — '

'No. Not yet. I'm really all right. I — I like it here. It's a different world I'm adjusting to, but it's good.'

'Why can't I come?' Her twin persisted.

'Because . . . ' Cressy hesitated. She didn't want to hurt her sister, to remind her, or fuel her guilt. 'Because, if you come up here, you'll make me remember.' It had to be said.

'Oh, Cressy! Do you mean I'm never to see you?' The wail was agonised.

'Don't be silly, Imogen.' Her twin's tendency to live life as though it was a soap opera was second nature. Cressy had always allowed for that, and defused the drama now. 'All I want is a little more time.' She was brisk. 'On my own.'

'But aren't you bored? What are you doing up there by yourself? It's so unlike you.'

'There's lots to do: reading, walking, looking after Montague. Flora Murray's a joy. I'm trying to — ' She stopped just in time. Her latest project was too new to discuss yet.

'I'm a bit lonely sometimes, but never bored — honestly. You'll be able to come soon. I'll call if I need you. I'm happy here. It's quite exciting — at times.' The image of the mysterious and attractive stranger swam into her brain, and with it, that elusive sense of recognition. the answer still refused to materialise. 'I've got to go, Imogen. I'll be in touch. Good luck with the play.'

Before she could put the phone down, she heard, 'Peter wants to see you too. What shall I tell him?'

'The same as before — to forget me. Nothing's changed.' Before her twin could protest, Cressy hung up.

She remained motionless, her hand

still on the phone. If only they'd leave her alone! What they did was out of love, she knew that, but her parents' concern, Imogen's guilt and Peter's hurt and bewilderment all pressed heavily, distracting her from recovery.

She thought calmly of the accident that had changed their lives. She was on her way to a rare Saturday morning shopping trip with her twin. They were walking along the pavement beside a busy road, chatting happily about the shopping to be done when, out of nowhere, a car tore straight towards them.

Cressida was behind and slightly right of Imogen. Positioned the other way round, maybe it would have been her twin at Quoyne House, and Cressida herself still in London. As the car hurtled towards them, Cressida automatically dragged both of them out of the way and threw herself on top of Imogen, shielding her from the worst of the debris. Her last memory was of the shattering, flying glass from the windscreen travelling towards her like glittering rain.

She'd simply been in the wrong place at the wrong time. Fate! It happened to hundreds of people. She and her sister were lucky — Imogen to be unhurt, and she to be alive and comparatively unscathed. A lot to be thankful for.

It was time to call her godfather. There'd be no pressure from Sir Ian. He'd always been mercifully brisk and businesslike, although his love for her was no less than her family's. She dialled one of his many numbers, and hit the right one first time. He was in his car, stuck in a traffic jam on London Bridge. Cressy could imagine it — sharp, horned irritation, exhaust fumes from a hundred airpolluting engines. Not for the first time, she was glad to be in the pure air of Pentsay, at the top of Scotland, as far away from London as possible.

'Cressida! Wonderful to hear from you at last. How's it going?' Sir Ian's sharp incisive tones had the same lilt as the stranger's.

Cressy's spirits lifted. What a wonderful godfather her parents had chosen for her. A multi-millionaire, Sir Ian Mackay had always been a significant factor in her life. when she'd asked to borrow Quoyne House for the duration, there'd been the merest flicker of hesitation before he'd agreed, packing her off with his blessing — and Montague!

'Great!' she reassured him. 'I've settled in now — the Murray's are fantastic. Montague is . . . um . . . very good company.'

'Shall I be coming up to see you? Do you want me to bring your parents?'

'No. Not yet, thanks. I'm enjoying my own company. Ian — do you know a man — broad, tall, Gaelic-looking — trace of Scots accent?'

'Fits most of the male inhabitants of Pentsay,' her godfather chuckled. 'Why?'

'Just — well, he was here earlier.

He knows you, and seems to know something about me — and Quoyne House.'

There was a pause. Cressy heard impatient honking in the background.

'Most people on Pentsay know a lot — or a little — about everyone. What they don't know they invent. I've often played that game. If he bothers you, tell Ben. He'll run him off. Now — Montague's behaving, I hope?'

The subject change was much too quick. Cressy's sensitive antennae. born of seven years as an investigative journalist, quivered. Ian wasn't being entirely straight with her.

'Ah, the traffic's moving at last.' Relief in his voice, he seemed anxious to finish the call. 'You're lucky to be up there, and not in this hell-hole.'

'Nonsense, you love it. I'll phone in regularly, now I've got my bearings. And, Ian — thanks. Quoyne House — Pentsay — is exactly right. You were an angel to let me have it.'

'Umph,' was the snorted response.

Cressy smiled as she put the phone down. Then the image reappeared in her brain. Where on earth had she seen that man before? She frowned into the mirror, and for once, seemed unaware of the puckered scar running from hairline to jaw on the right-hand side of her face. The frown deepened as she remembered he found a spare key! And why hadn't he returned it?

★ ★ ★

Next morning, Flora Murray telephoned to ask if Cressy would mind if she and her husband spent another couple of days on the mainland. Her daughter was ill, and the grandchildren were home from school.

Cressy missed Flora's company in the big house, although she was growing accustomed to being on her own, and enjoying it!

She planned a day's work sorting through her notes on the local stories

Flora had told her. A fine drizzle shrouded the long view from the house. Cressy turned up the central heating a notch, checked that the log basket was full, and settle down in the panelled study. Montague flopped round her feet, anxious brown eyes open, watching for any indication of the daily walk.

She would take him later, Cressy promised.

He thumped his tail and closed his eyes. Montague's future was beginning to worry her. In spite of his behaviour, she was growing fond of him — but Montague in her small London flat? She shelved the problem, to join most of the others.

After the accident, her mind had blanked, temporarily unable to grapple with the future. The trauma of skin grafts, plastic surgery and hospital, had been enough to cope with. One thing at a time, she told herself. Her career could wait. The long scar at the side of her face had put paid to a contract she had been negotiating with her

TV station, as anchor woman for a current affairs series. Her employers suggested that she either went back into investigative journalism or, sheepishly, they'd offered a back-room job in the news section.

Nick Burton, the programme controller, had been apologetic. 'It's tough, Cressy, but you can see — whatever you would be saying on the screen, viewers would be distracted by — er — er — your appearance,' he'd ended lamely.

'Make-up can do wonders,' Cressy had argued. 'Lots of bald people wear wigs.'

'This is different.' Nick had evaded her eyes.

'Why?' Cressy didn't feel different. She had the same keen eye and ear for a news story. 'The scar hasn't affected my brain.'

'You look — Oh, Cressida, don't make it so difficult. I don't want to tear up your contract, but I've no option. You've still got a job with us. It's just — '

'Just that I'm a cripple,' she said bitterly.

'Don't over-react. Take some time off — you've certainly earned it. Have a re-think.' He'd already started to dial a number — on to the next problem. Her time was up!

She was determined to beat self-pity, but it was hard when everywhere she looked she found that pity was reflected back at her. In Imogen's case, pity and guilt, which clouded her twin's flawless and perfect features. Cressy tried to make a joke of it — 'At least no-one'll have any problem telling us apart now,' she joked, trying one day to lighten her twin's gloom.

Imogen's tearful hysteria at that finally decided her. On the spur of the moment, she'd asked Sir Ian if she could borrow his island retreat for a while — Pentsay, with only the sea birds and sheep, was a place where no-one knew her, or cared what she'd looked like in the past. Maybe there she'd find a way to build her future.

Flora and Ben Murray's casual lack of reaction to her face when they met her on the mainland, confirmed the wisdom of her decision. Flora's main interest had been showing off Quoyne House, and later, when the two women became friends, entertaining her visitor with an endless stream of local legends and myths. Cressy's mind began to buzz — at last a project! And one she could work on, on her own. A new direction.

Absorbed, she worked solidly throughout the day, picking out the stories Flora had told her which might be suitable for children, then wrote a long letter to her ex-fiancé, Peter. Finally, she stood up, stretching her slim body, the late afternoon a gloomy grey, caused by a thickening mist sweeping in from the sea. It would be dark if she waited much longer.

'Right, Montague, patience shall be rewarded. Exercise — want to come?' No question. In one bound he was by the door, waiting for Cressy to put on her trainers and top. She bundled her long hair away from her face under an baseball cap. Not much chance of a viewing audience out there!

Dog and girl set off at a brisk pace, delighted to be released into the air, however damp. It was soft, clean, and smelled of the sea. Cressy swung into a faster pace. Ian Mackay's multi-gym and indoor pool had done wonders for her fitness. Her body felt supple and full of energy. Her feet were flying along a track skirting the fields leading down to a small loch about two miles from the house.

According to one of Flora's stories, it was home to a scaley, seven-toed monster which had frequently risen out of the mists to capsize the boats of those with the temerity to fish in its waters. Either that, or it simply reached in its multi-digit hand into the boat and reclaimed the fish. A good excuse for a poor day's fishing, Cressy thought sceptically, as she neared the shore.

She'd always wanted to learn to fish.

Maybe Ben would take her out one day — in spite of the monster! In the mist, the loch was ill defined, but she checked her speed as she saw, near to the shore, a dark shape on the pale water.

'Oh, no!' She'd have much preferred to run into the seven-toed scaley one, rather than the abrasively rude monster of the previous evening. He'd seen her, and was reeling in his line, taking up his oars to row in. If she carried on, the path would take her directly to his landing point — a narrow, wooden jetty, thrusting into the loch.

Abruptly, she turned and ran back the way she'd come. She thought she heard a shout, but ignored it and pounded away back up the track. Of all the ill-luck! Pentsay was about fifteen miles by twelve — big enough, she'd have thought, to avoid meeting the obnoxious stranger twice within twenty-four hours. She ran faster than ever, lungs and heart pounding with effort, her hair falling out of its restraining cap. Glancing back, the loch was well out of sight, with no sign of the man following her.

Slowing, she called Monty, who was streaking ahead. Too late, she realised the danger. 'Come back — AT ONCE!' she called, but he was gone, intent on the grey, woolly shapes in the field ahead. Usually, Cressy had him on a long leash when going past those fields, but the man at the loch had chased everything out of her head, except the importance of avoiding him.

Like a flash, Montague was over the stone wall, and among the sheep, barking gleefully at the prospect of the game he'd had in mind every time he'd passed the spot tethered on his lead.

Cressy vaulted after him, yelling frantically, trying to bring him to heel. The more she tried, the more he took her for a willing player in his game. The sheep bleated plaintively, running into each other, some of them trying clumsily to climb the wall to escape. Darting in and out, trying to catch the dog, she stumbled against the panicking bodies, and had a flash of homesick longing for the sheepless streets of London. Maybe she wasn't cut out for the country life after all, and would certainly be no shakes as a shepherdess.

A low-pitched whistle cut across the chaos. Monty stopped, ears pricked, head turned towards a broad figure emerging through the drizzly gloom.

'Get him out of here — of all the stupid things to do,' it shouted. 'Can't you see what he's doing?'

'Of course I can. I can't catch him,' she shouted back.

'You're making it much worse, flapping about like that.'

'I'm not — '

'Shush,' he snapped at her. 'Here boy — Montague — here.' His voice had dropped to a lower key and, miraculously, the dog trotted obediently towards him. the man bent down. 'Good boy — well done.' His tone sharpened again as he strode towards

Cressy, his hand twisted in Montague's collar. 'Your dog is far too young to be in a field of sheep without a lead. I told you yesterday that dogs who start to chase sheep don't last long. If it'd been a few weeks earlier, they'd have been lambing, and then there'd have been hell to pay.'

'I didn't send him into the field on purpose.' Cressy stood her ground, taking the expanding lead and snapping it on to the collar.

'Don't you know anything about the countryside?' Even in the gathering twilight, she sensed the anger in his face. 'If Stewart McCullock, on whose land you're trespassing, had come along, that would have been a dead dog — no argument! Once a dog's got a taste for worrying sheep, you might as well have him put down. But I don't suppose that would bother you — back to the city, without a thought for the mess you might leave behind!'

Cressy straightened up defiantly, facing the man, tossing her hair back. 'There's no need to be so aggressive. I'm not quite stupid. I know it's dangerous for the sheep. I always have him on the lead when going past these fields, but I . . . ' she stopped, unwilling to explain that she was running away from him — the glimpse on the loch.

'Yes,' he said grimly, 'I saw you run away. I guessed this would happen; the direction you were heading, the dog running free. I should have left you to it,' he repeated, still looking full at her.

'Why didn't you then? You seem to have a talent for interfering in my affairs. You can go back to your loch now, and leave us alone.' Cressy as horrified to hear the childish note in her voice, but there was something about the man's authoritative manner which made her feel like a schoolgirl — an unaccustomed sensation.

'I will — in a minute. But I'm not going without your word that you'll do something about the dog.'

'Why? What's it to you?' she was mutinous.

'Because,' he said more quietly. 'I like the dog, and don't like to see sheep harassed. Sufficient reasons for you?'

Cressy shrugged. Unfortunately, she could see the problem. It was impossible to keep Monty in all the time. The insufferable stranger was right, worse luck. If the puppy got shot, what would Ian think? Come to that, she'd miss Monty, too!

'He needs training. Can't you do it?' His question was scathing.

'I've tried,' she admitted, 'but I don't seem to have the knack.'

'I didn't suppose you would.'

'What's that supposed to mean? You know nothing about me.'

'I don't need to. Girl from the city — in the public eye — running way. I don't need to know anything more.'

Cressy gulped. 'That's the most dogmatic, prejudiced thing I've heard in a long time. How can you possibly make such snap judgements?'

41

He cut in. 'What I think doesn't matter. It's more important that you do something about the dog.'

Monty was straining against the lead, raring to get back amongst the sheep. Cressy took a deep breath and counted to five. It was a problem and she needed help. It went against the grain to ask him, but there was no alternative. 'Is there anyone on the island who could help me train him?'

He looked at her, this time a sweeping, comprehensive glance, which took her in totally, from baseball hat to the toes of her slim figure in its bright jogging suit. Still her scar didn't appear to register and, automatically, because she was thinking of it, she raised her hand and touched her cheek. In the gathering darkness, it was hard to tell whether or not she saw an imperceptible flicker, deep in the steely eyes.

'I could do it,' he said curtly.

'You? Why?'

'I've told you. I like animals. They're more rewarding than the human variety.

I'll give you half-an-hour a day. How long are you staying at Quoyne House?'

'I — I don't know. A few weeks maybe.'

A frown furrowed his forehead; he said harshly, 'You should go back south. There's still a lot of winter left up here. It can be bleak.'

'I don't mind.' Her reply was sharp. Who did he think he was, telling her what to do? She'd have liked to turn down his offer of help, but looking at Monty, she knew she'd no choice. 'I must be getting back. You're sure about the dog? Isn't there anyone else? I hate to bother you again.'

He chose to ignore the sarcasm in her voice. 'I said so, didn't I?' He put out a reluctant hand. 'Jon Grant.'

'Cressida Bellingham.' Their fingers touched briefly, and she felt the same heat as yesterday. A warm-blooded man.

'Sorry. I haven't heard of you.'

He said it with satisfaction, and

Cressy's hackles rose. 'Why on earth should you?' Yet she knew him from somewhere. If she could see him in the light!

He didn't answer her question. 'I'll be at the house at ten o'clock. Don't let him off that lead before then. he turned and strode away into the mist.

Cressy immediately ran off in the opposite direction — as fast as she could, putting as much distance as possible between herself and the abrasive mystery man.

3

Back at the house, she checked the locks, making sure that Montague was on the inside. Rummaging in the well-stocked kitchen cupboards, she planned a savoury risotto and a glass of wine on a tray by the log fire, in front of the television. Flora usually left her a meal, and Cressy hadn't had the heart to tell her she loved cooking and would have been glad to indulge in her hobby now she had the time.

The ambience of Quoyne House flowed around her. Originally, it had been a castle, dating back to the sixteenth century. Fire had destroyed its main core, but the nineteenth century laird who'd restored it had tried to follow the original design in miniature, but neither he nor his descendants ever had the money to make it entirely comfortable. Sir

Ian Mackay had bought it ten years ago, installing all modern luxuries, yet managing to retain its sense of historic grandeur.

The large bathroom was pure bliss, and she lay under several inches of foamy bubbles before supper. The relaxing bath was supposed to activate her memory about the mystery man of the loch. She knew somehow that the memory was a fairly recent one. She forced her mind back to the week before the accident. Apart from that horrifying moment of impact, she could remember very little. There'd been other victims, some of them more severely injured than herself . . . victims . . . Then, for some reason, the idea of terrorists came into her head . . . That was it! There was the connection.

She shot up, foam spraying over the deep-pile carpet as she leapt out of the bath, grabbed a thick bathrobe, and ran through into the bedroom. Jon Grant! Of course — full name Jonah Cameron Grant.

She'd brought some work files with her, to sort and clear. In one of them, there should be a full biography of Jon Grant.

Cross-legged on her four poster bed, she flicked through the file, with its photographs and cuttings on the life of Jon Grant, or Jonah Cameron, as he was known to the world. No wonder plain Jon Grant hadn't registered. Also, he looked very different from the pictures in the cuttings, especially the early ones which showed a much younger man, in spite of his trim beard. Expensively suited, in company with some of Britain's top industrialists, he was, in one photograph, shaking hands with the Prime Minister. The glossy magazines had displayed Jonah Cameron, brilliant, young entrepreneur at play, the escort of various glamorous women.

There was a picture, too, of his departure to the Middle East to tie up a successful business deal, on the steps of a jumbo jet, with a confident wave and brilliant smile over his shoulder.

Cressy's fingers hovered over the

cuttings. There should have been a blank sheet next, simply marked *504 Days*, before the next picture captioned *Released — after 504 days in captivity — hostage Jonah Cameron. Terrorists unexpectedly release the first Briton.* The photo duplicated his confident departure, showing him again in the plane's doorway. But this time, the joie-de-vivre was gone, the mouth grim, the face fined down — older. Jonah Grant was still a young man, but the dark, sardonic expression of the later picture had a bleak maturity which made Cressy shiver.

The final piece of the puzzle was in her diary, once an indispensable part of her busy life, unopened since she'd been on Pentsay.

Two dates were ringed round. One, Wednesday 10th, 2 p.m. — *Jonah Cameron's PA's office*. The other, the week-end before, simply said, *Imogen — opening night — Birmingham — theatre — meet for shopping — Saturday morning*. She'd never kept the appointment with Jon Grant's PA. He, himself, had refused to see her, or anyone else from the media.

Cressy remembered now, how helpful and co-operative he'd been with the press in the first few days of his return, particularly concerned for the hostages still held. Then, the scandal burst, and Press harassment had driven him back into another form of captivity. Hounded by journalists, avid for his reactions regarding the state of his business affairs, he'd disappeared completely from public view. She had been assigned by her TV station to do a piece on him, but her shopping date with Imogen had forced Jonah Cameron, or Jon Grant, out of her mind. He was the last person she would have expected to meet on the lonely island of Pentsay.

The financial papers attempted to analyse the collapse of Cameron Enterprises. Cressy become absorbed, then froze, as she heard a series of thuds. Montague, on the floor by the bed, lifted his head and growled, his fur standing up on his neck. There was silence.

Cressy had never felt nervous in Quoyne House before, even though Flora Murray had hinted at the possibility of unquiet spirits in certain parts of the house. No doubt the old walls had strange stories to tell, but Cressy was a practical sort of girl, and a firm believer in the here and now.

There was another thud — then silence. She listened hard. The sounds had come from the distillery, adjacent to the west wing of the house — right next to her room. The impoverished laird had tried to inflate the family fortunes by making whisky, but the distillery hadn't been used for years. She hadn't even explored it yet, but she was sure she'd seen its door was shut and locked when she'd checked the house. She put her ear to the wall. Unmistakeable sounds — there was something, or someone, in there!

Quickly throwing on a thick sweater,

jeans and boots, she picked up a flashlight from the kitchen, and cautiously unlocked the back door. Montague, for once, moved silently, a black shadow ahead of her. She crept quietly round to the front of the stone building which housed the whisky still. Lights shone from its small windows. Someone — not something! She wished she'd brought a weapon. The crowbar would have been handy — the knives in the kitchen seemed over-melodramatic — and dangerous! After all, the island was supposed to have no crime!

Taking a deep breath, she pushed the door open with her foot. Montague hurled himself into the room, and bounded up to the man over by the far wall.

'You! What are you doing?' Cressy asked in astonishment as Jon Grant spun round to face her.

It was the first time she'd seen him in full, electric light. He was far more attractive in the flesh than in the pictures she'd just been studying. The beard had gone, but thick, black hair curled around his ears, falling crisply over his forehead. She confirmed the strongly contoured planes of his face which led to a square jaw. Long, black lashes swept his cheeks, but his dark eyebrows, meeting almost in the centre, lent an aura of powerful masculinity to his appearance. His mouth was wide and sensuously lower-lipped, and his eyes, the deep, slatey, blue-grey she'd perceived before.

Unsmiling, he stared at her, automatically quieting the excited Monty with a small gesture.

'Our appointment was for 10 a.m., not 10 p.m.,' Cressy snapped, her nerves jangling with unease. 'Isn't it rather late to be calling?'

He shrugged his shoulders. 'I did ring the bell, but there was no answer.'

'I was in the bath. But, you've no right to be prowling round in here. What do you want?'

He thrust one hand into the pocket of his jeans, the other casually fondling

Monty's head. He continued to stare at her, unsmiling.

Cressy shifted her weight nervously. 'Well?'

'Well?' he countered.

'What are you doing here?' she almost shouted in exasperation. 'How did you get in — that door was locked — and it's late?'

'Not really. It's not ten yet. Early for city girls.'

'Will you stop calling me a city girl. Do you always stereotype people like this?'

'No.' Suddenly he smiled, and Cressy felt her stomach lurch. His eyes reminded her of the deep, dark waters of the loch. 'Perhaps we should continue our conversation inside the house — over a glass of Sir Ian's malt whisky?'

She took refuge in anger. 'You've got a nerve, and I'd hardly call what we're having a conversation. Why should I invite you into the house, let alone steal Ian's whisky?'

'You should invite me in,' he replied very deliberately, 'because you are responsible for turning me out — at very short notice. You may have found traces of my hasty exit in the master bedroom.'

'What?' Cressy's hand flew to her face. 'You were living in Quoyne House? I don't believe it. Ian would have told me.'

'Why should he? From what he said, I gather it was a sudden — er — whim on your part. I barely had time to gather up my things. Sir Ian was insistent, though I would have thought that the house was big enough for both of us to co-exist without a problem. But you apparently needed total solitude in which to nurse your bruised ego. The Murrays are here on sufferance, I presume. I always thought actresses would be fairly tough skinned.'

'I'm not an — ' Cressy began, then stopped. Why should she have to explain herself to Jon Grant? He

54

was impossible. She was glad she'd turned him out of Quoyne House. The thought of sharing it with him made her feel hot. She'd show him the door at once. Then she remembered Montague. He had to be brought under control. Jon Grant seemed to have a more subtle touch with animals than with humans. She'd wait until the training sessions were under way. It shouldn't take long, and she would pick up the knack quickly — then she could see Jonah Cameron Grant off the premises for good.

Also, the journalist in her was intrigued. What was he doing in Pentsay? After all the trouble surrounding his release, and the subsequent business disaster, he'd disappeared and no-one had been able to locate him. There were many unsolved questions hanging over him. As Cressy had told Nick Burton, she still had an eye and an ear for a good news story!

'All right, Mr Grant. I expect my

godfather can spare you a dram. Please follow me.'

Turning away, she snapped off the lights in the distillery, and led the way back to the house. As she went into the sitting-room she realised that, for the first time in weeks, she hadn't pulled her curtain of hair across her face before she entered a bright room.

Jon Grant was close behind her, too close for comfort, she decided, feeling a prickling sensation at the base of her neck.

'Shall I get the whisky? I know where it is,' he said quietly.

'No thanks, I'm quite familiar with my godfather's house and contents.' She resented the easy familiarity with which he moved around the room. 'Please sit down, Mr Grant.' Cressy was playing the formal hostess to establish her tenancy rights. 'I shan't be a moment.' She swept past him, and failed to see the twitch of amusement on his well-shaped mouth.

She fetched whisky and glasses from

the dining-room. He was still standing by the fireplace, staring down into the flames.

'I put a log on the fire. I hope you don't object.' He matched her formality, and Cressy nodded.

His tall figure looked entirely at home by the granite hearth, the firelight casting shadows on his strong face and thick hair which curled down onto the neck of his Aran sweater.

'Please,' she repeated, 'sit down.'

She poured a measure of pale whisky, and a much smaller one for herself. Never a spirit drinker, she'd yet to acquire a taste for the smoky peat of Sir Ian's favourite malt.

Jon Grant savoured his appreciatively. 'One of the things your godfather and I share. A taste for this. We often talked about getting the distillery going again.'

'So you know Sir Ian well? I suppose you'll tell me that's what you were doing tonight — planning to restart the still.' It was pointedly sarcastic. He was making her nervous. Her hands felt clammy.

'Yes, I know him well, and no, I've no plans at present to restart Quoyne House Distillery. Maybe in the future . . . ' He remained standing, looking down at her.

'Oh, do sit down.' Cressy was annoyed to hear her voice quaver.

'Am I making you nervous? There's no need, I assure you. I'm very respectable.' He came to sit beside her on the sofa.

Cressy wished he'd stayed by the fireplace. She jumped up. 'More whisky?'

'I've hardly started on this. Do you want to send me out rolling drunk?'

'No — I — ' She sat down. A log shifted in the fire, and she moved to push it back with the poker. Kneeling by the fire, with her back to him, she asked, 'Where are you living now?'

'The boathouse on the loch.'

'Is it comfortable?' She was beginning to regret the impulse that had invited him in.

There was a long pause before he answered. 'I've been in more uncomfortable places than the boathouse.'

'Ah — I'm sorry. Of course . . . when you were . . . er . . . in the . . . ' she floundered desperately.

A dark look of annoyance crossed his face. 'When I was held hostage. There's no need to be embarrassed about it. I'm not ashamed of it. I was, apparently, in the wrong place at the wrong time. It happens. Maybe that's how you got your scar. It looks like a recent injury. Wrong place — wrong time. I don't suppose it was your choice — especially in your profession. You'll be short of work for a time, I imagine.'

Cressy was stunned by his matter-of-fact tone. Most people shied away from even mentioning her injuries and, to her annoyance, frequently seemed to find her an embarrassment. Yet, she was perversely irritated by Jon Grant's bluntness. 'No, I wouldn't have deliberately walked into a shattering windscreen — but, the crashing car didn't leave me much choice.' Her voice caught in her throat, and she turned back to poke the fire violently.

'You'll have burns as well if you attack those logs like that. Leave the fire alone, it's fine.'

She spun round, green eyes blazing as furiously as the flames. 'Don't tell me what to do. And you still haven't explained what you were doing on the property.'

He stood up and drained his whisky. 'I don't have to explain anything to you, Miss Bellingham. This is Sir Ian's house, not yours. In fact, my rent is paid to the end of the quarter, so if I chose to, I could move back in — but, I won't — I promised your godfather.'

'No doubt he'll give you a rebate,' she flung at him. 'What else did you promise him — to keep an eye on me?' Her previous suspicions resurfaced. He must have a reason for hanging about Quoyne House.

'Keep an eye on you?' His voice was

genuinely astonished. 'What for? After your assault on me last night, I'd say you're perfectly capable of looking after yourself. What reason would there be for me keeping an eye on you — unless, of course, Sir Ian thought you'd be too soft for the rigours of our rough island life. You're city spoiled.'

'Don't be insulting. London's no soft option. It's much tougher there than here.'

'You are absolutely right on that.' He put his glass down. 'I'm curious. Why should you think I'm keeping an eye on you?' Moving to the fireplace, he stood over her.

Shakily, she rose to her feet, pulling back her hair. 'This?' She thrust her profile at him angrily, before releasing her hair to swing into its concealing curtain.

'So?' Jon's voice was puzzled. 'You've got a scar.' He put out his hand, took her chin, and turned her other side to him. 'This side is unmarked — and — more than reasonably presentable.'

Cressy jerked away.

'You're the most insufferably callous brute I've ever met. Please, if you've finished your drink, go!' Head flung back, she looked up at him and saw, reflected in his eyes, leaping points of flame and an expression new to her. It was an intensity she guessed was usually hidden behind the hooded eyes. She felt breathless as he put his hands on her shoulders, his strong fingers hard on her soft flesh.

He spoke calmly, but restrained anger grated in his voice. 'Self pity is not a pleasant thing. I reckon you've a lot to be thankful for. No, Sir Ian didn't ask me to keep an eye on you — just the reverse. All he told me was that you were a media star who'd had a bad experience, and needed a place to hide and recover.'

'So you assume I'm a neurotic, spoiled actress, wallowing in self pity, terrified of losing looks and career.'

'Something like that.'

'Well, you've got it all wrong. Your

prejudice is amazing. How would you know what it's like to be damaged?' In her rage, she forgot his background.

His hands still held her in a tight grip. She felt him tense. 'Oh, I do know what it is to be damaged, but I hope it doesn't warp the rest of my life. I don't think I was ever guilty of self pity — but, if it's pity you want from me . . . ' He bent his dark head to hers and kissed her.

Cressy stiffened, but a sudden swell tide melted her resistance. Jon Grant's lips were firm and warm, his hands moving down caressingly over her arms as his mouth continued to fuel the fire in her veins.

She reached up her arms, then let them drop, for her body simply refused to pull away. His arms moved up to her waist, drawing her closer to his hard body.

It had been a long time since a man had kissed her. Peter had tried, but it had been too soon after the accident. Mentally, she recalled her face, the first time she'd seen it after the bandages were removed. Disfigured! Ugly! That's how she always saw herself now — and that's how Jon Grant must be seeing her. His lips were gently teasing hers, and she realised why he was kissing her. Then she tore away, pushing against his hard chest with her fists.

'Stop it. I don't want your pity.'

He stepped away, and looked at her, grey eyes unfathomable. He said, very quietly, 'It's been quite a while, Cressida, hasn't it? I think it's time you faced your own hang-ups.' At the door, he turned. 'I can let myself out. Thank you for the whisky. And if you don't need my — er — pity, your dog needs my training. I'll see you in the morning.'

By the time Cressy had picked up a cushion and hurled it at his retreating back, the door had closed behind him.

Cressy stared at the door for some time after Jon Grant had gone. Damn him! How could he be so wrong? The last thing she wanted was his pity.

She went into the hall, and looked in the mirror. Large, green eyes, and a generously curving mouth in a heart-shaped face gazed back. A heavy fringe and long hair partly concealed the scar.

'You look like a moorland pony, or one of Monty's sheep,' she spoke ruefully out loud, lifting up the swathes of hair. Jon Grant really hadn't paid much attention to the blemish. Perhaps he had poor eyesight, but as she recalled the sharp intensity of his steely gaze, she was pretty sure he had perfect vision. Her lips remembered his mouth on hers, and the mirrored reflection showed a slow spreading blush as her blood raced. It had to be the shock of being kissed after such a long time!

She concentrated on tidying up, switching off lights and damping down the fire. The house still seemed to prickle with Jon Grant's presence. The background creaks and pings of central heating, and snaps of wood expanding and settling — all seemed abnormally loud. There was a restlessness in the house, as though the man's persona had called up kindred spirits from the past.

Quoyne House secrets were stirring, and Cressy felt a pressing sense of its history. The portraits on the stair wall and long gallery above looked down at her. She wouldn't have been in the least surprised to see one of the bearded, kilted lairds step down from the panelled walls . . .

'Don't be ridiculous, Cressida Bellingham. That man's muddled your brain.' His knack of materialising around Quoyne House was unsettling. Perhaps she was on her own too much. It was good that the Murrays would be back tomorrow.

She settled down to finish reading the Jonah Cameron Grant file.

After the first screaming tabloid headlines, most of the scanty news was in the financial press. The facts were stark. A couple of weeks after his release from captivity, a financial scandal had exploded in the city. Cameron Enterprises, thought, in Jonah Cameron's absence, to be under the safe management of his two partners, was declared bankrupt. The partners had disappeared, and the Department of Trade and Industry had called in the fraud division of the Metropolitan Police.

An ugly rumour slid out of the media back door, hinting obliquely that Jonah Cameron's capture and imprisonment had been a convenient disappearance to cover a wholesale transfer of company funds to undisclosed foreign bank accounts.

Cressy found it hard to believe the coincidence of the final cutting. Her office had kept the file on Jonah Cameron up to date. At first, she didn't notice the small item, ringed in red, at the foot of the page. That was because the main headline story was an account of that fateful Saturday afternoon when she and Imogen had gone shopping. The small news item at the base of the page simply stated, *Jonah Cameron, head of Cameron Enterprises, has apparently left the country — perhaps to join his associates in Spain or South America. The officer in charge of investigating the circumstances of the company's collapse refused to comment.*

Cressy's last thought, before she fell asleep, was what had Jon Grant been doing in the distillery?

4

Brilliant, blue skies and sunshine, the next morning, drove the uncertainties temporarily out of Cressy's mind. There was the first hint of the spring to come, and her spirits rose as she took Monty for an early morning run, over to the other side of the island where sheer cliffs rose out of the sea. She took great lungs full of the crisp, clean air blowing in over the North Sea. If only she could bottle it and take it back with her to London!

Suddenly, she found the whole notion of returning to London unappealing. She'd miss the exhilarating freedom of wide space and clean air. Eventually, she knew she'd have to go back. 'Not yet, though,' she called out to a passing sea bird.

The Murray's car was winding down the track to Quoyne House as she ran back with Monty. They all arrived at the house together.

Flora Murray, a petite, grey-haired woman, came to meet her. 'You're out early, Cressida. Are you all right?'

'Of course. I'm fine. How's your daughter?'

'Well enough, but we may have to go back again. I was a bit worried about you — '

'No need — really, but it's nice to see you. Let's have coffee. Or breakfast?' she added hopefully. 'I'm starving.'

'I'll put some bacon and eggs on. I've brought new-laid eggs . . .'

Flora began hauling boxes out from the back of their estate car, and Ben, her husband, came round to help. He nodded to Cressy, but he was a man of few words, and she'd accepted, that if it was gossip and conversation she needed, it would be Flora who'd provide it!

'Let me take some of those.'

She pulled out a box laden with

food, but Flora's sharp intake of breath stopped her.

'Ben — look.'

Husband and wife turned to look down the drive. Cressy didn't miss the warning glance that passed between them, as Jon Grant approached. 'But he's . . . ' Flora started to say.

'Hush. He'll know what he's doing. Morning, Jon. What brings you back to Quoyne House? You'll not have met Cressida Bellingham, Sir Ian's goddaughter.'

It was the longest speech Cressida had heard from Ben — proof of some agitation, she supposed.

Jon looked supremely fit and attractive in the sunlight, and a smile softened the stern lines of his face as he hugged Flora and shook Ben's hand. 'Great to see you both, and glad that you're back here. Don't worry,' he nodded towards Cressy, 'I'll explain later. Right now we have a problem dog to sort out. Come along, Cressida — we'll take him in the fenced paddock at the back.'

'Breakfast first?' she queried, without much hope. Jon's face had a determined look which spelled business.

'No thanks. Coffee later maybe.'

With a sigh, and a raised eyebrow at Flora, Cressy followed him.

★ ★ ★

Half an hour later, she had to admit he did have the knack. Montague was well on the way to being a reformed dog, and had shown a sharp streak of canine intelligence in speedily mastering trotting to heel, and the 'stay' command. She watched Jon Grant's patience and concentration with reluctant admiration. All his attention was focused on establishing a rapport with his pupil.

While he was totally absorbed in his task, she studied him openly. He posed a lot of unanswered questions, not least why he was so keen for her to leave the island, and Quoyne House.

'Cressida, your turn to do some

work. What are you dreaming about?'
Jon handed over Montague's lead.

'Sorry. I was miles away.'

'I thought you wanted help in training the dog yourself. You haven't been watching,' he reproved.

'I have — I — my attention just wandered. Let me try. It looked easy — the way you did it.'

'You've got to mean what you say. Establish who's boss.' Cressy was tall, but Jon Grant looked down at her with ease. 'In most relationships there's a dominant partner. Animals will respect you if you show authority. People, too!'

'There are such things as equal partnerships,' Cressida retorted.

'Not between you and Montague. If you want him to do as you tell him, you need authority. Here, take the lead, walk him up and down — use the same commands and gestures as I did, and every time you say his name — be firm.' He gave her the lead and turned away.

'Aren't you staying?'

'No. I'd only confuse him. There can't be two masters. I told you, there's only room for one dominant partner. Just stick to 'heel' and 'stay'. That'll be enough for one morning. I'm going to take Flora up on that coffee offer.'

Montague, of course, tried to bound after him, and Cressy had to turn her attention to controlling him, and transferring his oath of obedience from Jon Grant to herself.

It was hard work — much harder than it seemed when John had been doing it, but gradually Montague grasped the idea and seemed willing to give it a try although, after a while, they both lost concentration, and she called it a day. Her mind was on Jon and whether he'd still be having coffee, but Flora was alone in the kitchen when she returned, and the only evidence that he'd been there was an empty cup and saucer in the sink.

'He's gone?' Cressy thought he could have waited to see how she'd got on.

'Jon Grant? Yes.' Flora was busy at the sink.

Cressy poured herself some coffee from the jug on the hob, and perched on a high stool. 'Do you — have you known him long, Flora?'

'A while.'

'Does he come from Pentsay?'

'Round abouts.'

'Do you know how long he's staying here?'

'No.'

She sipped her coffee. Flora was usually talkative on all and every topic concerning Scotland in general, and the islands, especially Pentsay, in particular. Cressy felt she knew half the families there, even though she'd never met any of them! Jon Grant seemed to be the exception to Flora's rule.

She tried again. 'He tells me he was staying here in this house — before I arrived. He didn't seem to be too pleased about my being here.'

'Maybe not.' Flora kept her back to Cressy.

'Did you and Ben know that he's Jonah Cameron Grant?' she persisted. That brought a reaction!

Flora swung round, her mouth pursed. 'Yes, we do — but I can't answer your questions — and please don't ask any more, because I can't tell you anything. Mr Cameron Grant is on Pentsay to get away from all the mainland hullabaloo. He's one of us — and we protect our own against the world, and especially — journalists!'

The last word was spat out so venomously that Cressy was startled. She hadn't told Flora anything about her past job, and doubted now whether Flora would have been so free with her confidences before, had she known. Her godfather had vaguely indicated 'media', and the Murrays had come to the same conclusion as Jon Grant — that she was, or had been, an actress. It was a cover she decided to maintain for the present!

She looked at Flora's tight face. 'I'm sorry, I didn't mean to pry. I was just curious. He seems to have been around a lot in the last day or two, that's all.'

Flora's expression softened, and she came to sit down by Cressy, taking a mug of coffee for herself. 'Och — I'm sorry, too. I didn't mean to snap, but Ben and I were shocked to see him out here at all. We thought he wanted to be incognito, at least while he's — ' She stopped and looked distressed, then continued, 'Let's not talk about him at all. If he wants you to know anything, he'll tell you. It's his business and — ' she added warningly, ' — I don't think anyone around here would be very pleased if the Press or TV came snooping around. No-one on Pentsay is going to say where he is.'

The implication was clear! Cressy had been warned, she would be blamed, and would suffer the disapproval of the whole community. She was the outsider, after all.

She put the cup down on the sink. 'I'll be out of your way then, Flora.

I'm going to work in the study, then go for a walk. Don't bother with any food. I'll get my own supper.'

'As you wish.' The cold note was back in Flora's voice.

It was the first rift between them, and Cressy blamed Jon Grant, wondering what he'd said to Flora and Ben while she'd been working with Montague. Exasperated, she decided that she didn't care, and didn't want to think about Jon Grant at all. She had her own life to sort out, without getting involved in whatever he was doing — even though there could be a good news story attached to it. Forget it, she told herself, it'd only cause trouble. She remembered Flora's warning — probably she'd be held captive on Pentsay for ever, or thrown into the loch, if she broke the story about their precious, local boy's whereabouts!

★ ★ ★

Cressy flung herself into an active day, writing for an hour or so, then working-out furiously in the Quoyne House gym. She avoided Flora and Ben, spending the afternoon walking the island and testing out Montague's new guidelines. He was more responsive to her commands, although she didn't risk the sheep fields, making sure he was on the lead well before they reached them.

The gloriously sunny day was holding, and she was reluctant to go indoors. The thought of spending the long evening before her — alone — was unattractive. Maybe she would let Imogen visit. It would be fun to have her twin at the house, and to show her Pentsay. Sir Ian would be good company as well.

Cressy stopped. Ian had rented Quoyne House to Jon Grant, so he must know about him. He'd been very cagey on the phone, and she remembered his momentary hesitation when she'd related the idea of her flight to Quoyne House. A call to him that evening should pin him down to some answers.

She'd forgotten she'd decided not to think about Jon Grant. He seemed to have a dominating way of striding into her brain, and as she approached the track leading to the house, she blinked and stared.

He waved and came towards her. 'How was Montague?'

He bent and stroked the dog's head, and Cressy noticed his hands. Well-shaped, with long, strong fingers. Monty wriggled with satisfaction as the hands stroked and fondled the silky fur and Cressy felt a slow warmth spread through her — the glow of exercise, she told herself, dragging her eyes away from the sinewy strength of Jon Grant's fingers.

'Much better, thanks. You've worked miracles. You needn't have made a special trip to find out.'

'I didn't. I've come to take you out to supper.' He straightened up and

and looked her full in the face. 'The Murrays have gone. Flora was upset because you wouldn't let her cook your meal. So — I promised I'd see you had something to eat.'

'There's no need. Flora had no business discussing me with you. I'm happy to cook my own supper.'

'It was kindly meant,' he interrupted.

'I daresay, but I'm sure your mutual support system can find a worthier cause. I don't want your charity — or pity.' Her anger was rising at the notion of a conspiracy about her between the Murrays and Jon.

'I'm not offering either. I'm offering dinner! But if you're too proud to accept Flora's concern, that's up to you. She'll be disappointed. It's nothing to me.' He threw her a cold look and turned away.

Cressy flushed. He'd put her in the wrong, making her feel ungrateful and childish. Flora's motherly concern was genuine. Besides, Cressy wanted to blow away the coolness between herself and Flora as soon as possible. She'd come back hoping to see Flora before she and Ben left, to apologise. If Flora had asked Jon to take her out, it would only make things worse to refuse.

'Wait, please. I don't want to offend Flora — it's just . . . ' He came back towards her, 'I hate being treated like an invalid,' she ended lamely.

'But you're not. 'Nobody thinks you are — only you.'

'Some people . . . '

'Who?'

She hesitated, trying to think honestly and clearly. 'My family, I suppose — and some friends.'

'In London?'

'Yes.'

'This isn't London. I'd have thought you'd have realised that by now,' he said drily. 'So, you'll come then?'

'I — I don't seem to have much option.'

'A very gracious acceptance, Miss Bellingham,' he mocked. 'But it will have to do — if I'm to carry out

Flora's commission.'

So it was purely for Flora's sake he was asking her out. It didn't appear to be giving him any pleasure. The duty of one islander for another, she thought grimly.

'When do you want me to be ready?' she started to ask.

'Now, of course, while the light still holds.' He glanced at his watch. 'I reckon we've got an hour or so. My Land-Rover's parked round the back.'

'But it's only half past four.' Cressy was bewildered. 'Isn't it a bit early for dinner? And I'll need to change.'

To her intense annoyance, he threw back his head and laughed.

'What's so funny?' she snapped.

'You,' he replied simply. 'You don't understand. I've no intention of driving you for miles to eat at a fancy restaurant. You surely must have put two and two together to add up to the fact that I'm on Pentsay to escape public attention. No, Cressida, this is perhaps not the sort of dinner you're used to.' A splutter of mirth escaped his lips. 'And as for changing . . . ' he looked at her light-weight jog-suit and trainers, his eyes, pewter dark, lingering on her chestnut hair and slim, athletic body, ' . . . you'll need to change, but for this dinner date, you'll need a thick sweater and boots, or wellingtons. I'll give you five minutes, while I take Montague in and settle him down.'

Cressy stared at him, open-mouthed. 'Must you be so bossy?' she managed.

He came very close to her, so that she could see the tiny crinkles of laughter lines round his eyes. He must have laughed a lot — when he was younger . . .

'Go on, Cressida,' he said, giving her the gentlest of pushes. 'Five minutes. I told you this morning — someone has to be the boss.'

Ten minutes later, Jon Grant's Land-Rover was bumping down the track, away from Quoyne House, towards the loch and a golden, winter sun that still hung well above the horizon.

Cressy had abandoned all questions. If he wanted to make such a mystery out of obeying Flora's desire to see her fed, then that was up to him. At least it was a better bet than the solitary evening in front of the TV. That was beginning to pall, and it was nice to be out with a man again, and if bossy Jon Grant was the only one available on Pentsay, he'd have to do.

With a shock, she realised she'd not thought about the scar once all day. Nor had it registered when she was pulling on her thick Fair Isle sweater, and brushing her shiny hair. She stole a glance at the profile at her side, strongly defined, with a long, straight nose and high cheek-bones. It carried a stamp of power and decision. Not a man to be trifled with.

He turned and smiled at her. 'Relax. There's nothing to worry about here. You're not in competition for a plum part. No-one cares what you look like. You don't have to project a glamorous image. Be yourself for a change.'

'I always try to be myself,' Cressy bristled.

'That must be difficult — for someone in your profession.' His voice was sceptical. 'You don't have to impress me, anyway. Our only problem now is whether we'll be able to catch supper.'

'Catch it?' Cressy forgot her annoyance in surprise. 'Where are we going?'

'You'll see. We're nearly there — the outdoor annex of Quoyne House!'

They'd driven towards the loch, approaching it in a different direction from Cressy's usual walk. Now, as they dropped down towards it, she saw a tumbledown-looking building with a wooden jetty projecting into the water.

'That's not where you're living?'

'Where else? As you refused to share Quoyne House with me.'

'That's not fair. There was never any question of sharing it. When I came I had no idea anyone was already renting the house. Ian never mentioned it.'

'Well, of course he wouldn't. Come on, it's not as bad as it looks once you're inside. That's where we'll eat — providing the fish are obliging.'

He pulled up outside the boathouse and got out. Cressy followed more slowly, pushing away pangs of guilt. His eviction was nothing to do with her. He could have gone somewhere else on Pentsay if he'd wanted to stay on the island. No doubt many of the Islanders would have gladly given him shelter. She was curious to see inside, but Jon was making for the small dingy she'd seen before. It was moored by the jetty.

'Come on,' he repeated, 'before it's dark.'

It was certainly the strangest dinner date she'd ever been on and, after her initial surprise, she began to enjoy the tranquillity of the early evening. The sun, now winter red, was dropping behind the trees.

Jon rowed quietly out to the centre of the loch, and cast a line over the side.

He looked at her enquiringly. 'Want to try one?'

'I don't mind.' She tried to keep the eagerness out of her voice. He showed her how to bait the hook and hold the rod.

The evening was still, every ripple which lapped the boat making its own small sound. The water gleamed darkly and mysterious, and Cressy remembered the tales of the scaley, seven-toed monster! It seemed incongruous on such an evening, but the feeling of being suspended in a different world of time and place created the possibility of magic happenings. John was absorbed, his eyes intent on the water. She was sure he'd be a match for any loch monster!

Reality was more prosaic — and satisfactory. Jon caught two large, freshwater fish and, to her delight, she hauled in a small, rather odd-looking one which he said would be edible. They rowed back to the jetty as the stars began to appear in the purple dusk.

He moored the boat and carried up the fish. As Cressy, cold and stiff with sitting, stumbled on the jetty, he took her arm and held it firmly as he steered her towards the ramshackle structure. 'The restaurant's ahead.' he murmured.

The jetty petered out into a high shed. He led her through a door, and Cressy cried out in amazement. The large room was on two levels, like a barn, with a wooden staircase leading up to the second level. The lower room was softly lit with oil lamps, and a log fire in a stone hearth glowed and added its own light. But it was the furnishings which had made her gasp. A huge, soft, leather sofa was drawn up before the fire, thick drapes of a nubbly tweed covered the windows, and several rug skins were scattered on the bare-boarded floor. In one corner was a sink, cooker, and a long, pine work-bench.

Jon turned up the oil lamps, threw more logs on to the fire, and tossed the fish into the sink. He watched Cressy's reaction with narrowed eyes.

'It's lovely.'

He scowled. 'Lovely isn't the word I'd use. It can be pretty damp and chilly, but it'll do!'

'It's hardly primitive. You've even got a fridge.'

'Calor gas — and for the cooker. I never said it was primitive. I may be here for a while, so there's no sense in being unnecessarily uncomfortable. I've had enough of that.'

His grim tone stopped Cressy's questions. She went over to the fire to warm her numbed feet.

'Wine?' Jon opened the fridge. 'Supper won't take long. It'll be basic — but tasty.'

'I'd love a glass of wine.'

There was a long table in front of the sofa, and he brought glasses and bottle, placing them before her. 'Help yourself. Pour one for me, too. Meursault good enough for you?'

Cressy flushed. She wasn't sure whether the aggression in his voice was directed at her, or at some event in his past. She poured the pale gold wine into expensive looking crystal glasses.

'Rather over the top. Who are you trying to impress?' Her voice was tart.

He was at the sink, gutting and cleaning the fish. 'Not you, evidently. Don't worry, wine and glasses come from Quoyne House. Haven't you found the cellar yet? It's behind the distillery.'

'I know that. I've brought my own wine.'

'There's no need to sound so sour. It's all part of my deal with Sir Ian. Most of the luxury touches come from Quoyne House. I don't suppose you've missed them. The fish'll be cooked in a few minutes.' He brought plates, cutlery, tossed salad and crusty bread to the table. 'There's plenty of cheese and fruit if you're still hungry after the fish. Mustn't let Flora down.' He sat beside her on the sofa·and picked up his glass.

'I'm sorry you've had to go to

so much trouble.' Cressy said stiffly, moving away into the far corner. There were no other chairs in the room, apart from straight-backed ones.

'It was no trouble. I like fishing — and I have to eat, too.' He sniffed the wine appreciatively, and swirled it round in his glass. 'Drink up.'

She took a sip of the delicious white Burgundy. 'Your godfather has good taste. Did you know he's got some 1966 Lafitte laid down for you — I presume that's your birth year. I didn't touch that, of course — perhaps you'd like to share a bottle with me whilst we're both . . . imprisoned here?'

'I don't think so. It's for special occasions. And I'm not imprisoned. I wanted to come here.'

'We can always make up a special occasion,' he lounged easily on the sofa, long legs stretched out to the fire. 'You heading back for London, for instance, or . . . ' He leaned towards her and touched a corner of her mouth. 'Are you smiling for a change?'

She jerked away. 'I'll go back when I'm ready, and I do smile.'

'I hadn't noticed.' Jon looked at her gravely. 'Do you know how you look — most of the time?'

Cressy shook her head, avoiding his eyes, her brain in a whirl of confusion. 'The fish!' she cried desperately. 'It'll be cooked. I'm starving.'

He smiled lazily, and uncoiled himself from the sofa. 'All right, Cressida, we'll postpone the analysis until later. When you've eaten. You'll be more relaxed by then.' He poured some more wine into her glass.

The fish, baked in vine leaves, was deliciously flavoured with herbs and spices. She recognised basil and dill, but the accompanying sauce had an elusive flavour she couldn't identify. She had a healthy appetite and, it was true, she'd been starving. She concentrated on the food.

Jon Grant ate little, but kept her plate and glass full. 'I like to see someone enjoying their food,' he commented drily, as he made coffee and fetched a bottle of malt whisky from a cupboard.

'Not for me thanks, I've got some wine.' He'd been right, the meal had relaxed her. She leaned back with a contented sigh. 'That was truly wonderful. The best meal I've eaten in ages.'

His dark eyebrows rose. 'Surely not? Aren't you accustomed to the smartest London restaurants.'

'I'm not. I don't know what sort of life you think I lead — or led before.' She swallowed. 'Anyway, you're wrong as usual. It's not like that at all.' She tried to steer the conversation away from herself, 'Why are you on Pentsay, anyway. Don't you have unfinished business in London?'

His face darkened, but he answered without hesitation. 'Yes, I do — but I have unfinished business here, too. Business which doesn't concern you.'

'It does. You want me out of Quoyne House. Why?'

'Have I said that?'

'No, but it's quite obvious.'

'To you maybe . . . '

'How do you know I won't inform the police — or the Press — where you are.'

'What? A holiday — back to my roots. Not much in that.'

'It's more than that.' Cressy sat upright, he was maddeningly evasive.

'Why are you staying on at Quoyne House?' he countered, stopping her next question.

'Isn't this obvious?'

'That you're hiding away from the world — yes. Why — is more difficult.'

'Can't you see?' she cried.

He put down his glass and moved nearer to her. 'What I see is an exceptionally beautiful woman, with perfect features, magnificent sea-green eyes, a very desirable mouth, and, I imagine, an equally desirable body.' His black-lashed, grey eyes held hers hypnotically, and Cressy was conscious of his arm laid behind her, along the top of the sofa.

His voice was persuasively gentle. 'Also, Cressida, you're capable of deep emotions, which you take great care to hide behind a prickly manner which isn't natural to you. You've hardened yourself to all feeling. It shows in your face, denies your beauty. You've got to learn to smile again . . . to trust . . . '

Cressy clapped her hands over her ears. 'Don't! Don't! Stop it! It's not true. How dare you — how can you say I'm — desirable — attractive? It's all ruined.' She was trying to accept it, and beginning to succeed. It was wicked of him to raise her doubts — and hopes.

'Rubbish.' He took her hands away, and cupped her face in his hands. 'You're exaggerating. You're just frightened, just scared to let yourself go — like this . . . '

He drew her towards him, and began kissing her gently. She went rigid, but his touch, remembered from the previous night, fired her blood. His hands caressed her body, and the intensity of his kiss deepened. She felt his answering flame as he drew her down on to the sofa.

He leaned away from her for a moment, and the leaping flames of the fire highlighted the burning intensity of his eyes. Her eyes fastened on his lips curving above her. Desperately she wanted him to kiss her again. Ashamed — and shameless — she pulled him to her.

'Cressy,' his voice was strange, 'don't.'

He moved away from her, and she stiffened. So — he couldn't bring himself to touch her — a kiss was as far as he could go. She felt dizzy — angry and sick. With a violent push, she slid away from him and stood, shaking.

'You see — it does make a difference! You can't, can you? You can't bring yourself to kiss a cripple!'

He looked stunned. His eyes glazed, then sparked with anger. He stood up and faced her. 'Is that what you really think? A cripple! You don't know what cripples are. You're totally obsessed with yourself. It's time you grew up and stopped running away. Try thinking of other people for a change.'

'Like you, I suppose. You're running away as well — remember! You're hiding, too — avoiding your responsibilities — a coward! At least I'm answerable to myself, and not a whole load of creditors.'

She picked up her coat, snapping the Velcro jerkily in her anger. 'I'm going home. Thanks for the supper. I'll tell Flora you've done your duty. I've been fed — and counselled. A pity it didn't work. I'm not as gullible as you seem to think.' She hurled the words at him and made for the door leading to the jetty.

He stood up, his face dark with anger. 'If you go that way, you'll end up in the loch. Don't be such an idiot. I'll drive you back.'

'No thanks, I prefer my own company. I'll walk.'

'No doubt — but I'll complete my duty if you don't mind. Flora would never forgive me if you fell in the loch.' He grasped her arm, and led her through another door. 'Though a ducking is what you probably deserve,' he gritted, more or less dragging her to the parked Land-Rover.

'No you don't,' he added as she tried to break free. He held her with one hand, wrenching open the passenger door with the other. He bundled her in, slammed the door shut, ran round the other side, and had started the engine before Cressy had time to find the unfamiliar door handle. Revving the engine, he screeched the truck round, and drove up the track towards Quoyne House.

Cressy pressed herself against the door, as far away from him as possible. She hated herself — and him. He'd been playing with her, seeing himself as the good guy who could bring herself to terms with her disfigurement — but naturally, he couldn't go through with it! Her carefully built-up pride was shattered.

They were at Quoyne House, and she heard his exclamation, 'What on earth?'

She looked up. The house was ablaze with light. The front door opened as their tyres crunched to a halt, and Montague came bounding up to meet them. Simultaneously, they leaped out of the Land-Rover, and both ran to the house. At the front door they stopped. Cressy was in front, but she heard Jon's sharp intake of breath behind her. In the hall, clearly seen in the full light, was her replica — except that the hairstyle was a close-fitting, chestnut cap, and the face was flawlessly unmarked!

Imogen ran to meet her with a cry, arms flung out to hug her twin. 'I just couldn't stay away any longer. I'm sorry, I had to see you.'

Cressy went into her twin sister's arms, but not before she'd turned to Jon Grant, who was staring at Imogen as if transfixed. 'Now,' she said to him. 'Now, do you see?'

5

'No, I don't see — but I do recognise Imogen Bellingham, the actress. She must be your twin sister.' Jon stepped forward and held out his hand as the twins released each other.

Imogen looked enquiringly from Cressida to Jon, now well defined by the porch lights. She clapped her hand to her mouth and gasped, 'You're Jonah Cameron Grant — the hostage — who came back, and then disappeared . . . when . . . '

'Well spotted.' Jon didn't seem at all put out by the instant recognition. 'It took your sister a lot longer. Not that I want to be recognised,' he added hastily, 'but I'm amazed I missed the likeness.'

He turned to Cressida, and she saw how much younger he looked, his face was alight with animation, all trace of anger vanished. 'Your face was familiar, but it was your sister. I saw Imogen in Edinburgh, at the Festival Cabaret. You were terrific.' He turned his full attention on Imogen, who automatically responded with a flashing smile of appreciation and pleasure.

'But that was ages ago, at least two years. Cressy, why didn't you tell me Jonah Cameron Grant was with you on Pentsay?'

'I didn't know. I — we — only met a couple of days ago.' Cressida could hardly believe it was such a short time.

'She had no reason to tell you,' Jon cut in swiftly.

'But — Jonah Cameron Grant! You're hot news on the mainland just now.' Imogen looked puzzled, and Cressida saw that she hadn't let go of Jon's hand. 'Don't the police want . . . ?'

'Imogen!'

Cressida's warning cry was lost as

Jon brushed aside Imogen's question, ushering them inside. 'Let's go in. There's no point in freezing on the doorstep. I'd say a visit from Imogen Bellingham calls for a bottle of champagne. I know just where Ian keeps it — I'll replace it from stock later.' He took natural charge as host, and when they were all inside the huge, baronial hall, Cressida thought resentfully he was acting as though he still lived in Quoyne House.

Montague's excitement subsided to a regular tail thumping, and he obediently sat on Cressida's command.

'See, it's not difficult to establish who's boss. He's yours for life now. This was one wild dog only yesterday,' Jon explained to Imogen. 'Cressida's tamed him.'

'Cressida! She doesn't know a thing about dogs. And I still don't know why you're here, Mr — er — Cameron Grant.'

'Jon — please!' Again he ignored her question. 'Champagne — it's in the cellar. I was quite a fan of yours, Imogen, after that Festival. You were the most spirited actress I'd seen in years. I suppose it runs in the family. You two go into the sitting-room, and I'll fetch the wine.'

'In the family?' But Jon was already out of earshot.

Imogen collapsed gracefully onto a sofa. 'Cressida, just what is going on? I was worried about you being here alone, and now I find you with the most attractive and interesting man of the decade. No wonder you don't want company.'

'Don't be silly — '

'What is he doing here, and where've you been tonight? You both looked very agitated when you screeched up the drive.' Imogen's eyes, just a shade darker than Cressida's, sparkled with curiosity. 'Do tell me — was it a romantic assignation on the loch by moonlight, or a gallop along the beach, or . . . ?'

'You're an idiot. I haven't found a

beach yet, nor seen any horses, and there's certainly no romance between Jon Grant and me.' She tried to fight the rising tide of colour flooding through her as she remembered his kiss. Impulsively, she hugged her sister. 'I'm glad you're here — and I've no idea what he's up to. Apparently, he was renting Quoyne House before I came. He's not too pleased I'm here, but I'm not giving him the satisfaction of turning me out. I like Pentsay and I like Quoyne House. I'm staying!'

'Good for you! I think this place is more than just a bit spooky — all those ancestors on the walls. They seem to me to be a pretty dour lot.'

'They're all previous landowners — lairds. There's some fascinating stories. I'll tell you tomorrow — and about my new project.'

'Tell me now — and — I've a letter from Peter for you. He wants to come and see you.'

Cressida closed her eyes. The outside

world again — impinging — bringing more problems.

'Cressy? You'll have to talk to him . . . '

'Not now, Imogen, please. Wait until Jon Grant's gone. Better still — tomorrow.' Then she realised what had been bothering her since her sister's arrival. 'How did you get to Quoyne House?'

'Plane. Ferry. Taxi . . . '

'No. How did you get into the house?'

'Walked in. How else? Monty met me by the door. He was very friendly and we came in together.'

'I locked the door, I'm sure of it — and Jon put Monty inside while I got changed . . . '

'He must have escaped, and you must have forgotten to lock the door. If I was going out with Jonah Cameron Grant I'm sure locks, keys, and dogs, would never enter my head. I just assumed that in a place like this doors would always be left open. There can't be many burglars around, they'd be too conspicuous . . . Where's that man with the champagne, I'm dying of thirst here.'

Jon's deep voice interrupted her. 'Sorry — mission failed. I can't get into the cellar. The lock's jammed. Have you been down there Cressida?'

'No. I told you, I brought some wine with me, and Ian left plenty in the kitchen racks. There isn't any champagne up here, though.'

'Oh, never mind.' Imogen jumped up impatiently. 'Wine'll do — or, maybe, a small dram? I loved Uncle Ian's malt specialities when I tried them in London.'

'A girl after my own heart.' Jon was already by the small bar in the corner of the room. 'What about you, Cressida?'

'Nothing thanks. I've already had wine tonight.'

'Quite a while ago,' Jon murmured, his grey eyes holding hers with a wry smile.

'I'll go and make coffee,' she stammered, unnerved by the smoulderingly slate glance.

'Spoilsport,' her sister teased, accepting a crystal tumbler from Jon with a long-lashed flutter.

Cressida quickly left the room. She knew Imogen couldn't help it. It was part of her actress make-up, and second nature, to flirt with every man who crossed her path — but did she have to lay it on so extra thick for Jon Grant? Cressida banged the coffee mugs unnecessarily hard on the work top. She wondered again about Imogen getting into the house. It still bothered her. She was sure she'd locked the door before she went out — but had Jon followed her, or had he been already outside? The man had so confused her brain that she couldn't think straight any more!

The water took an age to boil. She gave Monty a drink, and settled him into the utility room for the night. Sir Ian had decreed the dog should stay outside, and on the first night, Cressy had tried, but Montague's anguished yowls under her window had torn at her soft heart. Monty's aim was to sleep on her bed, but they'd finally compromised on the utility room. That was near enough the back door for Montague to pretend he was a real guard dog.

When she returned to the sitting-room with the coffee, Imogen and Jon were laughing and chatting like old friends, side by side on the sofa, Jon's arm laid along the back, his hand within touching distance of Imogen's bright hair. Cressida put the tray on a coffee table, painfully aware of Jon's keen scrutiny.

He looked from her to Imogen, shaking his head in amazement. 'You're so alike, yet so different. It's fascinating.'

'Of course we're different.' Cressida swallowed. 'I should have thought that was obvious, especially now.'

Jon replied evenly. 'I wasn't meaning your scar. I'd forgotten you were so paranoid about it.' A shocked gasp from Imogen brought him round to face her. 'Isn't it time you all accepted it? Cressida will never make progress if you treat her as an invalid with some awful disability.'

'We don't.'

'I don't want to talk about it.'

The girls had spoken simultaneously, and Jon gave an exasperated sigh. 'OK, OK. I'll finish my whisky and go.'

'Drink your coffee.' Imogen put a hand on his arm. 'You never saw Cressida — before. It's harder for us.'

'She's the same person, for goodness' sake!'

'As twins, we've always tried to be different.' Cressida desperately tried to shift the slant of the conversation. 'We made a pact when we were six years old to dress in different styles. Clothes, hairstyles, make-up — we've a strong bond, but even when we were very small, we instinctively sought our own individuality. We're separate people . . . '

110

'My hair changes colour at least twice a year . . . '

'Imogen always wanted to be an actress, whilst I . . . ' Cressida stopped and bit her lip.

' . . . am not!' Jon finished for her. 'So your twin tells me. You certainly fooled me. Well, what do you do?'

'Didn't Imogen say? I used to be a journalist — and I didn't fool you. You leaped to the wrong conclusion.'

'Used to be?'

'I was about to go into television — on network news programmes.'

'Ah!'

'So, you see,' Imogen rushed in.

'No. I may appear obtuse, but there're plenty of other areas in journalism — if you really want to stay in that — er — profession.' He said the last words with bitter distaste.

Cressida bristled. 'It's really none of your business what I do, or did.'

'Hey — what's the matter with you two? This is meant to be a celebration.

Have some more whisky.' Imogen went to fetch the decanter but Jon put up his hand.'

'No thanks. I'm going. How long are you staying?'

'I've got to be back for Saturday evening's performance. That gives the understudy a good run. Oh, I forgot to tell you, Cressy, Uncle Ian's coming up on Thursday — for the day. Literally a flying visit. Says he wants to see you, and there's some other business — he was pretty vague about. Do you know Sir Ian, Jon?'

'I do.' All trace of previous laughter had gone, and his tone was grim. 'I look forward to seeing him again.'

'You'll be seeing him? I thought you were here incognito.' Cressida was sharply abrupt.

For once Jon Grant looked discomfited, but all he said was, 'I am — on the whole.'

There was an uncomfortable pause.

'Well, I shan't give you away!' Imogen put in brightly, in an unsuccessful effort to ease the tension.

Jon tossed back the last drops of whisky and stood up. 'It's time I went. Tomorrow, or Friday, if the weather's good, I'll take you both round the island. We'll have a barbecue on the other side. It's more sheltered there.'

'I don't — ' Cressida began, but Imogen's reaction was swift.

'That would be great. Just what I need, huge gulps of fresh, clean air. Isn't it a brilliant idea, Cressy?'

In the face of such enthusiasm it was hard to disagree, but already Cressida felt cast in the role of third party, and she was annoyed that Jon Grant had preempted her plan. She'd been looking forward to showing Imogen around her favourite island spots. 'Very kind,' she said, with a touch of frost.

Jon frowned. 'If you've got other plans . . . '

'No. Come on, Cressy, it'll be fun,' Imogen pleaded, unwittingly casting her twin into the spoilsport role again.

'I've said — it's kind. If the sun's

out tomorrow, I'll ask Flora to pack a picnic.'

'Good-night then, Bellingham twins.' Jon's gaze raked both girls, but it was Imogen who caught his hand and saw him out.

Cressida slowly cleared the mugs and glasses onto the tray. Imogen's clear laugh and Jon's deeper answering one floated on the air before the front door slammed, and her twin whirled back into the room. 'He is really nice! I could stay on a few weeks if Jonah Grant's here.'

'He'd like that, too, from the look of things. He's desperate to be rid of me.'

'Oh, Cressy, that's ridiculous. You never used to be so touchy before — ' she broke off, ' — the accident.'

'At least Jon Grant's right about that. I wish you'd stop tip-toeing around it. I do need to talk — to be normal about it. Don't you see, that's why I had to come away, and be on my own. Look, Imogen.' She drew her hair back from her cheek. 'It's still there. The scar won't go away. I'm accepting that, but when you come and talk about the accident in that hushed tone, I remember it all again. It's heaven here. Flora, Ben — they don't even seem to notice, and as for Jon Grant — '

It was Cressida's turn to stop in mid-flow. Wasn't she throwing back his very argument, his attitude, to her sister? He'd ignored the scar and treated the situation abrasively. Wasn't that what she wanted? Not pity? Perhaps his embrace hadn't been pity, and she'd mis-read it. Could he possibly see her as quite normal, even find her attractive? But how could he, especially with Imogen's unmarked beauty for comparison?

'What is it, Cressy?' Imogen looked concerned.

'Nothing. I don't know. I'm a bit confused — tired, I expect. It's been quite a day. Don't look so serious, Imogen, it doesn't suit you. It's late — we'll talk in the morning.'

'I don't feel tired, but you're right. Let's get up early and go for a walk. There's lots I have to tell you — and — don't be angry, Cressy, but can we talk about more surgery. There's a new technique.'

Cressida put her hands to her ears, but smiled as she did so. 'I'm not quite ready for that. But I promise, when and if I am, you'll be the first to know.' She held out her hand, and the two girls went up the wide, oak staircase side by side, with the long line of Pentsay lairds frowning down at them. 'I'll tell you about them, too,' she promised as she showed Imogen to the sumptuously luxurious bedroom next to hers. 'I'm truly happy you've come,' she reassured her still anxious twin. 'Honestly.'

'I'm glad I came. Cressy — don't you like Jon Grant at all?'

'Not at all,' she lied, unconvincingly.

It had been a long day and Cressida fell asleep in seconds, but fitful dreams disturbed her. The recurring nightmares of the accident had mostly been

116

exorcised by skillful counselling. The major problem remained. Her physical disfigurement had led to mental uncertainties. She no longer perceived herself as a successful career woman. Her rejection by the TV studio had left her insecure, unsure of everything about her life. At Quoyne House she was beginning to unravel the snarled up threads of her existence and think about new directions — a new persona. Ironically, Jon Grant, by his careless acceptance of her disfigured looks, was pointing the way forward, and she was genuinely happy to see her twin. She felt no envy towards her at all. But she wasn't ready to leave Pentsay yet!

Feverishly, she tossed and turned, murmuring in uneasy sleep. The lairds in the portraits edged up from her subconscious, emerging as terrifying dream images.

One of Flora's many stories had been the legend of Gordon Kinross, who had shot his young wife's lover to death, and drowned his faithless bride in the loch. The nineteenth century laird, all powerful on the small island, wrote the murders off as 'accidents', but the young man's family meted out its own justice by waylaying the savage laird and battering him, as they thought, to death. Gordon Kinross survived, but lost his sight and much of his reason.

His portrait was at the head of the stairs, and Cressida had often shivered as the sightless eyes seemed to follow her with a demonic stare. Flora had told the story well, and with relish, ending with the warning that 'Gordon Kinross still roams house and grounds searching for his assassins, tapping his way with one of the boughs which felled him'. As most of Flora's yarns finished with a ghostly presence coming back to haunt its tormentors, Cressida wasn't alarmed. She was a girl of stout heart, and didn't have the over-developed imagination of her twin sister.

But now, in her nightmare, through the dark, pre-dawn woods behind Quoyne House, the ghostly laird chased her past the inky loch, through the fields of surreally gigantic sheep, and up the drive of the house. The door was open. Cressida laboured to reach safety, pursued by the clumping stick and the swishing black cape of the portrait. Gasping for breath, she fell on the doorstep just as the door slammed shut before her, leaving her outside at the mercy of Gordon Kinross.

She screamed and, with a thumping heart, shot up in bed, trying to stifle the cry of fear lingering from the nightmare. Hands wet with sweat, she fumbled for the light, snapping on the switch. Gordon Kinross faded in the reassuring familiarity of the room — but that door slam — it was so still real, as were the soft rustlings.

Cressida got up, went to the window and looked out. Pitchy, black clouds raced across the sky, playing hide and seek with a fitful moon, and as Cressida looked down the driveway, she thought she saw a dark shadow coming towards the house. With her hand on her throat she peered into the garden. The moon disappeared, and so did the figure. Had that tall form been enveloped in a cloak? Had there been anything there at all?

Far away in the distance a solitary light glimmered on the hill.

The house was so still it seemed to be holding its breath, but as she turned back into the room, the silence was sharply fragmented by angry barking. Montague, shut in the utility room, had found a new voice. It wasn't his usual hopeful yelp of hurt neglect meaning 'why couldn't he be with Cressida upstairs'. She'd never heard this sound from him before and it made her blood race. Montague's bark was a full-bloodied, guard dog roar of alarm — and it was not meant to be ignored.

6

Cressida and Imogen came out of their rooms simultaneously. 'What on earth's the matter with the dog?' Imogen, still sleep-drugged, clutched her sister's arm. 'Burglars?'

'Not very likely, they'd have a terrible problem getting in.' Cressida remembered her own difficulty too well. 'You go back to bed, and I'll go down and see.' She tried to speak calmly.

'Not likely — I'm coming with you. Ian's probably got a gun somewhere. Shall we look for it?'

'Imogen! This isn't a scene from one of your thrillers. I'm sure we're quite safe. Montague's probably having nightmares.'

The barking was already subsiding as they made their way downstairs, but increased in volume when they let him out. He greeted them energetically, making constant dashes and frantic sniffles against the outside door.

'He just wants to go out.' Imogen sounded disappointed.

'No, it's not only that. He thinks there's someone out there.'

'Don't open the door. You might let them in.'

Cressida bit her lip. Montague was big, black and fearsome-looking to someone who didn't know he was a softie, but if she let him out he might get lost, and she wasn't as confident as Jon Grant about his new found obedience. Fortunately, he calmed down completely, and just looked pleased to have some company. 'I think we'll leave him. Whatever — whoever it was, seems to have gone.'

'Do you think we should do a house search?'

'I'm sure no-one could get into Quoyne House,' Cressida repeated. 'It's burglar proof. There's even an alarm system, but I asked Ben to switch it off. I set it off a few times by mistake, and it goes right through to the local police. I've had them up here twice.'

'Why did Ian go to so much trouble? It's so remote here.'

'There's a lot of valuable stuff in the house, and his main home's in London remember. There's much more likelihood of a break-in there, although that's impregnable too. Scottish caution, I guess.'

'Maybe he got a good deal — two burglar alarm systems for the price of one.'

'That's not as far fetched as it sounds. Ian loves a deal! Do you want some coffee, now we're up?

Imogen yawned widely. 'No thanks. I'll go back to sleep. How about you?'

'No. I'll just re-check the locks. You go on up.'

'Are you sure? Shouldn't I come with you?'

'I'll take Montague around with me. He can sleep on the landing for the rest of the night.'

'He'll love that.' Imogen said sleepily. 'Good-night again — and — Cressy, do you know, that for the first time since it happened, I've not noticed your scar.'

'That's because my hair covers it.'

'No, that's not it. I don't know . . . '

'Don't worry about it. Try and get some sleep.'

Imogen went upstairs, and Cressida checked the locks, the bolts on the doors, and windows. She hesitated by the door leading to the cellar steps. It was at the end of a short corridor off the kitchen. She'd never been into the cellar itself, although Ben had offered to show her around. He'd told her it was a vast, underground room running the entire length of the house, with lots of nooks and crannies off the main vault, and that there was an exit out into the grounds which was never used, totally overgrown with trees and bushes. Cressida resolved to check that out the following morning. It was a possible way into the house if both cellar and corridor doors were unlocked — which wasn't very likely given Sir Ian's passion for security.

She had no intention of braving the cellar, even with Montague in tow, but she unbolted the corridor door and peered down the stone stairs. She put on the light, relieved it was so well lit. It all looked very ordinary and she went down the steps with only a slight tremor of nervousness. The massive, solid door looked impenetrable. The key was in the lock but, as Jon Grant had said, it was jammed there solidly. Cressida could turn it neither to the left or right, but at least it was totally secure. It would need tools of some sort to shift it.

She wondered if her godfather kept anything of value in the cellar apart from his fine wines. It was safe anyway, and that was her main concern — there couldn't possibly be anyone in there. Montague confirmed this because, after a desultory sniff or two, he turned away, uninterested.

She left the hall and stair lights

on, picked up a heavy old-fashioned poker from the living-room just in case, and went upstairs with a delighted Montague at her heels. She avoided looking at the portrait of Gordon Kinross in his black cape!

'Stay!' she commanded the dog outside her bedroom door and, to her amazement, he stayed. Jon Grant had wrought a miracle.

Jon's voice was the first thing she heard far too early the next morning. The bedside phone rang and she picked up the receiver, still half asleep. 'Mmm . . . ' then, 'Cressida Bellingham here.'

'You don't sound very alert! Have you looked outside your window yet?' The deep voice, with its slight, musical Scots lilt, squeezed her heart, and she was instantly awake.'

'No.' She struggled upright, blinking at the clock. It was only eight o'clock.

'The sun was up at dawn, but it's pouring down now. The barbecue's off — we'll try again on Friday. When does

Imogen actually leave?'

So that was why he was ringing so early — her twin was obviously on Jon Grant's mind. 'I don't know. Probably not until Saturday morning. She may even hitch a lift back tomorrow with Sir Ian.'

'And you, Cressida?'

'I'm staying.' She wondered whether to mention the noises of the night. Maybe he had heard or seen something odd. 'Jon, could there be burglars on Pentsay?'

'Why do you ask?' His voice was sharp.

'Last night — Montague made an awful racket, and I — I thought I heard a door slam. You didn't see anyone, anything — on your way home?'

'No.' His hesitation was fractional, before he said swiftly, 'You should have Ben and Flora live at Quoyne House. It's too isolated for a couple of women. Better still, you ought to go back to the mainland.'

'That'd please you, of course.'

'I'm thinking of your safety.'

'But it is safe here. A lot safer than in London.'

'Maybe. We'll see what Sir Ian has to say about it. Did anything else happen last night?'

'No. I wish I hadn't told you. I certainly shan't tell Ian.'

'I shall though.' Jon's voice was grim. 'He phoned me half-an-hour ago. He's asked me to lunch at Quoyne House tomorrow, but I'll come over today to check over the house and grounds, and ask Flora and Ben to stay.'

Cressy exploded in frustrated anger. 'You will not! I can't undo Ian's invitation, but you take too much on yourself, Jon Grant. I don't need Flora and Ben to live in. They've got their own family problems, and I'm very capable of looking after myself thank you.'

'What about Imogen? Have you thought of her safety?'

'Of course I have. We're not a couple of kids. There's nothing to worry about.

Good heavens, one barking bout from Montague . . . '

'All right, Cressida, don't get so steamed up. I'd like to come and see you anyway.'

See Imogen, you mean, Cressida thought angrily. 'And I'd like the day to myself with my sister. We'll see you tomorrow.'

'And Friday for the barbecue, if the weather's good — or I'll cook you dinner in the boathouse if it's raining,' Jon persisted.

Cressida sighed. 'Let's take one day at a time. I hate being organised,' she added pointedly.

Jon had recovered his good humour, and his soft laugh sent shivers through her. 'You're a very intriguing and fascinating woman. Also a very obstinate one. You're quite a challenge, Cressida Bellingham!'

'I am?' Her voice rose in surprise. 'Don't you mean Imogen?'

'Oh, yes, Imogen especially.' The laughter deepened. 'I'll see you both tomorrow then — and, Cressida, put the burglar alarm on.'

'How did you know that there is a burglar alarm, Jon?'

'I lived there for a while, remember. And it's fairly prominent — on the wall outside — as a deterrent.'

'Did you have it on when you were here?'

'No.'

'Then, I won't. Goodbye, Jon.'

She put the phone down feeling that she'd scored a point, albeit a childish one, and settled back into bed to think about him. Cressida was no fool, and always tried to be honest with herself. She was attracted to him, but it was an attraction she must fight. She was physically scarred, and he was interested in her sister.

She got up, fetched a hand-mirror back to bed, and subjected her face to its closest scrutiny since the accident. When the bandages had first been removed, she'd insisted, against all advice, on looking in the mirror.

'You're still so bruised. You'll soon look a lot better. Leave it for a while.'

'Now,' she demanded.

With a pained air, the doctor had briefly flashed a glass in front of her. That had been his mistake the brief glimpse of her swollen distorted face, with its still broken nose, had so horrified her that she refused to look again for weeks, and for ever after, even after her nose had been re-set, and the bruises and cuts healed, she'd retained that grotesque image in her brain. She remembered, too, the dismay in Peter's face — a dismay which he quickly hid, assuring her that it didn't matter, she was still Cressida, the girl he loved and always would.

Poor Peter — Cressy felt a dreadful pang, and dreaded reading the letter he'd sent via Imogen. He was so good and loyal, yet she couldn't convince him she really didn't love him. The accident had been the catalyst. For months before she'd been uneasy. They'd grown up together, drifted into a relationship, and become engaged, but she was sure that they were both beginning to feel their affair was more akin to a comfortable old dressing-gown than a glamorous ball-gown. But for the accident, a mutually friendly end would have not been far off. Now, she was sure Peter felt morally obliged to stand by her. She'd broken off the engagement, but he was hard to get rid of. She knew now that she was right — Peter had never ignited her senses in the way Jon Grant's merest touch did.

She took a long hard look in the mirror.

The left side of her face was relatively unscarred. An inch long cut merged into her eyebrow. Her nose, which she'd considered hideously out of shape, looked surprisingly normal, with the tiniest bump near the bridge. Her wide mouth looked fine from the left. She turned her head and saw the long, jagged scar again. After countless operations and grafts, it was the best the surgeons could do, and she had to admit they'd done a miraculous job. It certainly couldn't be ignored, and it had pulled up the side of her mouth slightly, but it was well past her right eye and back towards her hairline. When her long hair concealed the right side of her face, no-one could tell she'd ever been in an accident.

'Cressy?' Imogen's voice at the door was tentative.

Cressida laid the mirror down and smiled. 'Do you know, it's not that bad after all.'

Imogen's whoop of joy as reward enough. She leaped on to the bed and hugged her sister until Cressida cried out for mercy. 'At last! Now we can talk about it.'

'Now, perhaps, you can stop feeling guilty.'

'I'll never stop feeling guilty.'

'Just because we were in different positions? But let's forget it. I want to show you Quoyne House. There's a pool and a gym — we'll have a workout before breakfast. You'll meet

Flora and Ben. We'll go walking, even though it's raining.'

'What about Jon Grant?'

'He phoned. The barbecue's off, but he's coming to lunch tomorrow with Uncle Ian.'

Imogen's face had dropped, but brightened at the latest news. 'Let's make the most of today then. I've lots to tell you: there's an offer of a part in a TV series, the play I'm in may go to New York after the West End, and I want to hear about your plans . . . '

★ ★ ★

The two girls never stopped talking all day. Cressida felt as though she'd been released from some immense burden and, for the first time, Imogen felt she could be her own natural, bubbly, uninhibited self.

Flora and Ben were charmed by Imogen. Ben was more talkative than Cressida had ever known and even joined them for lunch in the kitchen.

Cressida had warned Imogen not to mention Montague's alarm in the night and, even though it was a dour day of sagging grey cloud and rain, the night-time fears receded before the cosy luxury of Quoyne House by day.

In the afternoon, the rain almost stopped and the girls took Montague for a walk to the nearest bit of coast. Cressida told her twin about her plans. 'It's stories — for children. Flora told me so many tales, legends, and myths of this area. As she talked, I could see the characters so clearly. They kept popping into my head, and I found I was doodling and drawing them as she told me the tales. I think I could even illustrate it myself. There are sea-monsters, mermaids, trolls and hobgoblins — and tall, fierce, mountain men . . . '

'Sounds scary to me,' Imogen shuddered.

'Children like to be scared a bit — remember Snow White and her wicked stepmother — '

'I had bad dreams about her for years.'

'My characters aren't as scary as that. For instance, there's the mountain man who comes out of the mist to lost travellers. Flora's legend has it that if you see him you never find your way home again, and that you die on the mountain and get eaten by gryphons . . . '

'Don't,' Imogen shrieked, 'and there's no such thing as a gryphon — '

'There aren't any mountain men either — but my mountain men are going to be kind and helpful to children in distress. I've done a lot of work already. I'll show you when we get back — and all areas of the world have their own legends. I could do a series. Look, here's my favourite bit of coastal path.' Cressida strode on, hands thrust deep into her jacket pockets, her face turned to the sea, long hair streaming behind her.

'Hey, slow down, I'm not as fit as you.' Imogen puffed behind her.

'OK. Take a look at that view.'

'Take a rest is better.'

The cliffs were steep on this side of the island and rose sheer out of the dark pewter sea. The lighter grey cloud rolled to the horizon edges as far as the eye could see.

'A symphony in grey,' Cressida said. 'It can totally change colour when the sun's out — and be a symphony in blue!'

'Look,' Imogen pointed out, 'there's a yacht out there. A big one.'

'It's been there for a few days. I saw it last week-end.'

'What's it doing?'

'Whatever yachts do, I suppose. Cruising the islands — it's a bit early for the tourist season, but maybe they're serious bird watchers — or fishermen maybe? Let's go back. It looks like more rain. Flora's been baking madly for tomorrow's lunch, and there's always tea and crumpets by the living-room fire!'

'Can't wait. I've had more than my

ration of fresh air for one day.'

The time slipped by. Flora had made cakes, scones, and pies, and Imogen and Cressida forgot about sensible eating, sitting by the fire, sampling the delicious home-cooking. Later on, sipping wine and talking endlessly, they watched the news on television and then went to bed. Exhausted by the exercise and pure air, and the lack of sleep the previous night, they both slept like logs.

★ ★ ★

Out in the North Sea, the tall yacht, with lights dimmed, edged as close as possible to the shoreline before anchoring. A rubber dinghy, rowed by one of two black-clad figures, pushed away from the sleek side and landed by the inlet where a path led up from the beach — a path which eventually led directly to the back of Quoyne House.

Montague, back in the utility room,

twitched in his heavy slumber. He'd had a long walk, and this time failed to hear the almost imperceptible sound of a key turning in the front door. This time, the door closed silently behind the two dark figures. They crossed the hall, stopped at the bottom of the staircase, and looked up. Like black statues, they waited for about ten seconds, then one figure nodded and pointed forwards. Stealthily, they moved towards the corridor leading to the cellar, watched only by the austere eyes of generations of Pentsay lairds.

7

'It's hard to believe it's taken you girls twenty-six years to see Quoyne House!' Sir Ian Mackay, a tall, well-built man with a shock of iron-grey hair, carved the roast saddle of local venison that was the main feature of Flora's gourmet lunch, lovingly prepared in honour of the current Pentsay Laird.

'I wish I'd come before,' Cressida took her plate from him, 'but now I've discovered it, you won't get rid of me very easily.' Concentrating on laying down the hot plate, she missed the significant look that passed between Jon Grant and Sir Ian.

The small party of four made only a small demand on the seating capacity of the long, oval table. Jon Grant sat next to Cressida, and she was nervously aware of him so close to her. As he handed her a tureen of vegetables, their fingers touched and her nerve-ends tingled.

She'd finally read Peter's letter that morning and, to her intense relief, he had accepted that their relationship was over, and he released her from all obligation. He wanted to see her, and to remain friends, and she was glad of that. She sensed he'd met someone else and that pleased her, too. Her new freedom made her more than ever conscious of Jon Grant. Part of her wished he would go away, back to the boathouse, but the other part somehow longed for him to stay.

They were all served when Sir Ian casually remarked, 'You're looking so much better, Cressida. Isn't it time you thought of coming back to us in town. London's not the same without you there.'

'I'd like you to come back, too.' Imogen added, ' 'Dance of Time' is transferring to the West End soon — we can be in the flat together. I'd love that.'

Cressida had a large, comfortable flat in Highgate which Imogen shared when she was in London.

'You can still use the flat,' Cressida said hesitatingly, 'but I'd like to stay here for a while. Not because I don't want to go back to London — I'm almost ready for that, but I'm working on something and I need to be on Pentsay.'

Sir Ian's eyebrows rose. 'Working? Here?'

She had no option. She had to explain about her new project. There was no point in keeping it secret.

When she'd finished, Sir Ian nodded approval. 'Great idea, Cressy. Well thought out.'

'But surely you've got all your material now — from Flora? Do you have to stay at Quoyne House to write the stories?' Jon Grant sounded angry.

'I want to.' Cressida flashed him a resentful look. 'I want to use Quoyne House as a base — to visit the other islands, and the mainland.' She didn't add, it's none of your business, but her tone implied it, and the tension between them hung in the air like an icicle.

Jon shrugged his shoulders and shot a questioning stare at Sir Ian, who said slowly, 'You know you're always welcome at Quoyne House, both you and Imogen, but I have to say that I'm planning a series of business conferences here pretty soon. Would you want to be around then?'

Cressida's heart sank. It was quite obvious that Sir Ian wanted her to leave. For some reason she couldn't guess at he was aiding and abetting Jon Grant. The two men had spent an hour before lunch, closeted in Sir Ian's study, and had emerged with absorbed and serious expressions.

Her godfather went on, 'In fact, I could take you and Imogen back to town today. You could be home by teatime.'

Sir Ian had piloted his own light aircraft, landing in the field behind

Quoyne House, which had a specially built runway and helipad.

'Today!' both girls chorused in unison.

'Well, Imogen's got to be back on Saturday, so I thought she may just as well fly back with me.' Sir Ian sounded tentative — very unlike his usual, decisive self.

Cressida was bewildered. The sudden urgency to get her off Pentsay was unnerving. Something odd was going on. 'Ian, if you want me off Pentsay today, just say so, and I'll go and pack my bags now. But there must be a reason. Can't you tell me what it is?'

This time Cressida was watching closely, and there was no mistake. Sir Ian glanced at Jon, whose tiny headshake was negative.

Her godfather arrived at a decision. 'There's nothing. Stay as long as you wish. Now — how's that dog behaving, and is all well with the house? Are you using the gym and the pool?' Sir Ian's brisk change of subject caused a black frown from Jon Grant.

She ignored it. 'It's great. I'm getting into good shape. Montague, thanks to Jon, is a changed animal. He's perfectly obedient now, and I'm going to hate leaving him — when I go.' She looked defiantly at Jon, but he was staring moodily at Imogen. 'One thing I forgot — the cellar door's jammed. Not that I've needed to go down there.'

'Well I do! I want to take some wine back to London. I'll get Ben on to it straight away. And there's a change of plan. I'll stay here tonight and fly back first thing tomorrow. There are quite a few things I need to organise here at Quoyne House. You'll stay for supper, Jon?

Before Jon could reply, Flora came in with coffee, and Sir Ian spoke to his housekeeper. 'Wonderful meal — as ever. Jon and I'll have coffee in my study please, Flora. And could you make sure Ben's around, I need to see him. Would you girls excuse us?'

Flora nodded, poured coffee for

Imogen and Cressida, then carried the tray away. Jon and Ian followed her.

'Well!' Imogen exploded, 'You're right, there's something going on. Suddenly Ian is carrying on like a campaign general! Do this, do that — what's it all about?'

'I haven't the faintest idea, but we've no choice but to let them get on with it. You and I'll go out and walk off that delicious lunch.'

The sun was out but the sky looked threatening when they came out of the house. Cressy hesitated. 'I think I'll take a waterproof, too. Shan't be a minute. I'll catch you up.'

As she crossed the hall, she saw that the library door was not closed properly. Raised voices were clearly audible. Dare she eavesdrop? After all, whatever was going on involved her at Quoyne House. Feeling very guilty, she tiptoed to the door.

Jon was speaking, his tone urgent. ' . . . impossible with the girls here — they'd be banking on an empty house.'

'I can't order Cressida away. You can see, the more I say, the more determined she is to stay. I think you're over-reacting. Ben's here. What possible harm could come to them?'

'It's just so much more difficult — it may even be dangerous. They'll stop at nothing. And I think we're very close . . . '

'Why don't you tell Cressida?'

'No.' Jon's voice was firm. 'She's a journalist, don't forget . . . and if she broke the story . . . '

'She wouldn't — '

'I don't trust — ' His voice dropped. 'Where are they, by the way?'

'Out for a walk. Don't worry.'

'That door's not shut — '

Cressida turned and fled, slipped out of the front door and ran after Imogen — without her waterproof.

'Sorry,' she gasped, as she caught up with her sister, 'I'm afraid I stayed to eavesdrop on Ian and Jon.'

'Cressy! That's not like you.'

Well — they won't tell us — and something's happening — both of them are in on it. Maybe we should leave Pentsay, and you certainly should. Why don't you go back with Ian in the morning?'

'And miss Jon's barbecue! No thanks. You don't get rid of me like that.'

'I don't want to get rid of you. You're welcome to Jon Grant, but he said, whatever it is, might be dangerous — '

'All the more reason for my staying. Why don't you come back with me on Saturday?'

Cressida's thoughts were in turmoil. She wanted to stay. She wasn't particularly afraid, but she didn't want to upset her godfather. If he really wanted her to go, she would. She'd tackle him in private later to see if he could give her some inkling of what was going on. 'Perhaps I will,' she conceded.

As it happened, there was no opportunity for a private talk with

Sir Ian. When they returned from their walk, there was no sign of either of the men. Flora told them that Sir Ian had spent most of the time on the telephone, and then he and Jon had gone off with Ben. They'd be back for supper.

Meanwhile, the cellar door had been dealt with, the lock unjammed, and the key back on the main house key-ring. Flora was in her element; delighted to be cooking for more than just Cressida, and no, she didn't need any help. Why didn't the twins have a swim before supper?

Imogen loved the indoor pool, where the water was kept to a warm seventy-five degrees, and the Jacuzzi was bubbling hot. 'Call me five minutes before supper — I'm going to enjoy this bliss for as long as possible.' Her voice was a languorous murmur above the pounding jets, and Cressida laughed affectionately.

'OK, but don't go to sleep. I want to go to the library. I'll give you a call before supper.'

'Mmm,' was the only reply.

Cressida was prepared for the fact that she might have to leave Quoyne House. She'd probably got as much out of Flora as she could, but Sir Ian's library had a wonderful collection of books on local myths and legends, and she hadn't yet exploited its full potential. If she could borrow a few books to supplement Flora's material, she could finish the first series of stories in London. But she hated the idea of leaving Quoyne House and Pentsay. She'd always thought she was an out-and-out city girl, but the island had cast it's spell on her, and she wondered if she could ever really settle in London again. Her life was taking on quite new directions.

She showered and changed and, for the first time since arriving at Pentsay, chose to wear a dress, the only one she'd brought. It was a softly draped, jade-green silk which enhanced her hazel eyes and set off her dark, chestnut hair. Its clinging folds showed a figure of breathtaking perfection. High-heeled sandals gave her added height. Jon Grant was very tall — but she pushed away the notion that she was dressing to impress him, or compete with her flawless twin. In a defiant gesture, she lifted her hair away from her face, and secured it in a high pony tail, so that it was no longer masking her scar.

The library was warm and cosy. A log fire smouldered in the hearth, and Cressida gave a sigh of pleasure. How she'd miss the comfortable, quiet luxury of Quoyne House! She went to the shelves, and picked out a couple of books. The other one she wanted was on a higher shelf. She stretched up on tiptoe — it was just out of reach.

'Let me.' The familiar voice was by her ear, and a strong arm brushed hers. 'This the one?'

Cressida daren't move — he was so close. One small movement and they'd be touching. 'Yes,' she gulped, seeing the familiar gold lettering on the leather bound spine. He moved away. Holding the book, she stayed motionless.

'Well turn round, for goodness' sake. I'm not going to eat you.' Jon Grant's voice rippled with amusement, and slowly she turned to face him. He caught his breath in a gasp of amazement, and Cressida's hand flew to her scar.

She felt a warmth rising from her toes as he carefully put down the book he was holding and came towards her.

'Cressida . . . you're beautiful . . . ' His grey eyes, silvered by the light, were fringed with long, dark lashes, his mouth soft, slightly parted, showing strong, white teeth, his cream, soft wool, casual sweater enhancing the outdoor ruggedness of his face.

Cressy took in every detail of him before she found herself in his arms, and he bent to kiss her. She knew she should struggle, break away — but it was impossible. Her body, so long starved of physical tenderness, responded with a will of its own. She clung to his masculine frame like a lifeline, and his kiss, exploring sweetly, was as tender as she could have imagined, his hands caressing her shoulders and neck, his fingers moving up her cheek, her right cheek . . .

She drew back sharply. 'No, don't,' she cried, her mouth hating to leave his — but the unaccustomed touch on the scar had startled her.

'Why not,' he murmured, drawing her back into his arms. 'Does it hurt?'

'No . . . ' she stammered. 'It's just — so — so ugly!'

'It's not at all. That's just in your own mind.' He looked deep into her eyes, holding her attention with a mesmeric stare. He spoke thickly, and Cressida could feel the tension in his body, and her own reaction. 'If you hate it so much, you could minimise it even more — ' He hesitated, kissed her softly on the mouth, and said. 'I have a friend, a cosmetic surgeon in Edinburgh. I've told him about you. I could make an appointment. He'll see you straight away. Ian could fly

153

you there tomorrow, before he takes Imogen — '

Disappointment, despair, and anger, flooded through her. Yet another ploy to get rid of her! Was there no length to which he'd go? Kissing her, flattering her, softening her up for the kill. She pushed him away and stepped back to put as much distance as possible between them.

'Why don't you just drop me in the loch?' she cried childishly. 'That way you'll be sure to be rid of me. There's no need to express this bogus concern for my welfare. Very convenient to have me put in hospital — I expect your precious surgeon friend would be sure to recommend an immediate long-stay operation. No thanks. Mr Grant. It won't work. I'm not leaving Pentsay now.'

His head jerked back as though she'd slapped him hard across the face. The soft, sensual expression vanished and his mouth tightened. Eyes, now a dark angry pewter, snapped back at her.

'You really think I'd go to those lengths to get you off the island. I took you for an intelligent woman, a courageous woman who seemed to be sorting her damaged life out into new directions. I was wrong. You don't deserve help.'

'I don't want your kind of help. Why don't you go back to your boathouse? Leave me alone.'

'I'm a guest of Sir Ian's. He's invited me to supper, and I'm staying.'

'So am I,' she flung back over her shoulder as she ran out of the room.

Taking deep breaths to calm herself, she went to call Imogen. All she could think of was how she could get through the evening ahead with Jon Grant. His presence, so close to her, would be exquisite torture — but no-one must know it. She thought of a way.

Her sister was back in the pool. 'Imogen, it's nearly supper time. Jon Grant's here, and he's looking pretty devastatingly handsome. Why don't you put on your best outfit and really go to town on him?'

Imogen's look of surprise quickly changed, and the light of challenge shone in her eyes. She hauled herself out of the pool and grabbed a towelling robe. 'How long have I got?'

'It's about half an hour to supper,' Cressida replied brightly, fighting back her tears, conscious of an awful numb pain spreading round her heart.

The plan seemed to work. Jon came to the meal looking thunderous, and Sir Ian was preoccupied, but Flora's cooking, Sir Ian's wine, and Imogen's vivacity and beauty, honed directly on Jon, melted away the atmosphere. Imogen's performance was superb.

By the end of the evening, Jon was pledged to go to London to see her first night appearance, when the play transferred from the provinces. The fact that he was wanted by the Fraud Squad for questioning regarding his business affairs seemed to have entirely slipped his memory. He hardly spoke to or glanced at Cressy during the entire evening, and she was fervently thankful when, at an unusually early hour, she could plead a headache and go up to her room, to give way to tears of frustration and despair. It was very late when she heard Jon's Land-Rover crunch away down the drive, and Imogen's bedroom door close.

The other watchers from the yacht, returning a third time to Quoyne House, had seen the aeroplane on the runway, the Land-Rover in the drive, and the lights blazing from within. Uncertainly, they stood deep in the shadows of the granite walls, then, after a whispered consultation, silently started back to the yacht.

8

Did Jon Grant ever sleep late, Cressida wondered as she and Imogen dragged themselves out of bed just after dawn to see Sir Ian off. Jon was at Quoyne House having a very early breakfast with her godfather. The two men looked serious as the girls joined them for coffee.

'This is disgustingly early.' Imogen, drooped over the table, made them all smile.

'The best time of the day. The sun's coming up, and it may rain later, so enjoy it while you can.' Sir Ian put a folder into his briefcase and stood up. 'I'm off. I've an appointment in the City at one-thirty.' He drained the last of his coffee and looked at Cressida. 'Are you sure you and Imogen won't come back with me? I can wait a few minutes.'

'No, of course not. I thought we'd all agreed — '

Sir Ian cast a significant look at Jon. 'So be it. Keep in touch then. And, Cressida, I'd rather you switched the alarm system on. It was expensive enough to install. No point not using it.' He kissed Imogen, then Cressida, giving her an extra hug. 'Glad to see you looking so much better.'

She hugged him back. 'That's Quoyne House, and Pentsay. All thanks to you. I promise I'll be back in London soon, but I want to come back here often.'

'I hope you do,' Sir Ian said gruffly. 'Now, Jon, you see me to the plane, and we can finish our chat. You girls stay here. Go back to bed if you like.'

'I thought we had a barbecue planned,' Jon said. 'The morning's perfect. We'll start as soon as I've seen Ian off.'

'Wonderful,' Imogen enthused, suddenly discovering an early morning vitality.

'I don't think I'll come,' Cressida

said quickly, 'I want to finish off some work.'

Ian and Jon were already at the door. 'See you both in London,' were Sir Ian's final words.

Imogen poured more coffee. 'Cressy, you've got to come. It's my last day. Why don't you want to?'

Cressida couldn't find an adequate reason that would satisfy her twin. How could she confess that her feelings for Jon were so ambivalent that it seemed best to avoid him altogether. Especially after last night!

But Jon appeared to have forgotten the tensions of the previous evening. When he came back to the dining-room he was brisk and cheerful. Like a tour guide operator, Cressida thought resentfully as he hustled them into action, ignoring her protests that she would prefer to stay at home.

'Rubbish,' he scoffed, 'I promised a tour of the island, and this is our last chance. Imogen leaves tomorrow, and it's a glorious, Spring morning. All the picnic stuff is in the Land-Rover.'

'Flora will be annoyed — '

'Stop creating difficulties, Cressida. Flora provided the food — I'll cook it! We leave in ten minutes. See you outside.'

'What power,' Imogen breathed admiringly, as he went out.

'Unbearable bossy boots,' Cressida complained.

At this, the two girls burst out laughing, and that set the tone of the morning.

It was as though a truce had been declared. The bright spring sunshine was irresistible, and the Land-Rover swept down the drive with the two girls sitting up front with Jon, an excited Montague bouncing around in the back. Cressida exclaimed in surprise at an enormous bonfire Ben was attending away in a distant corner of the grounds.

'Spring clearance, I expect. Ben's extending the vegetable garden,' was Jon's answer to Cressida's query, as they left Quoyne House behind.

Pentsay was only fifteen miles long, but its odd, irregular shape gave an extended coast-line. Cressida had not driven much, preferring solitary walks from Quoyne House, so she was fascinated, in spite of herself, by Jon's tour.

He was a knowledgeable and charming guide, and set out to entertain them both with a running commentary of the island's flora and fauna. He drove around the coastal tracks, starting at the clifftop side, then dropping down past the tiny fishing village and harbour, which was Pentsay's main centre. A handful of colour-washed houses, a post office, and a pub, fronted the harbour wall.

Imogen wanted to stop and take pictures, but Jon vetoed that. 'I'm not particularly keen to be seen around the village at the moment. We'll make for a sandy beach I know, a few miles away on the other side of Pentsay.'

The cove was a sheltered hot-spot,

ideal for the barbecue which Jon organised with effortless efficiency. They ate, drank, and lazed on the beach, throwing sticks for Montague, and skimming stones along the shiny surface of the sea. Far out to sea, some fishing boats took advantage of the calm weather.

'The yacht.' Imogen pointed to the horizon. 'It's moving off.'

Jon fetched a pair of binoculars from the Land-Rover, and watched until the yacht was a distant speck.

'It was over the other side before,' Cressida said, as Jon eventually lowered the glasses. He turned away, but Cressida caught a look of dark bitterness on his face as he went to clear up the barbecue.

'Must we go?' Imogen asked in surprise, when he began to pack up the equipment, 'it's fun here. And so warm you could almost swim.'

Jon laughed. 'I wouldn't risk it, it'll be freezing. And,' he jerked his head at the sky, 'the weather's about to change.

We've had the best of the day. There's a storm coming.' Indeed the clear blue sky of the early dawn had given way to a rolling, black, cloud mass in the distance. 'We'll get back, and then you should batten down the hatches and stay indoors for the rest of the day.'

Cressy left the pretty beach reluctantly. There had been a holiday mood to the morning, reminiscent of childhood picnics — a relaxed and carefree atmosphere which had been a welcome hiatus to the tensions she usually felt when Jon Grant was around. They climbed back into the Land-Rover.

The light-hearted mood had vanished, and Jon drove them back to Quoyne House. He deposited them unceremoniously on the front doorstep, seemingly in a hurry to leave. 'Don't forget to switch on the alarm — and Ben will be living in, until you leave — no argument.' He stopped Cressida's protests before she could utter them. 'I'll pick you up tomorrow morning, Imogen, and take you to the ferry.'

There was a spatter of rain and gusty wind as he jumped back into the Land-Rover and drove off.

Both girls were left with a feeling of anti-climax after that. They went down to the gym and pool, then settled by a blazing fire, chatting and reading.

As dusk fell, the rain which had been driving down all afternoon, eased off.

Montague had been restless for some time, so Cressida decided to brave the elements and take him out for a short, brisk walk.

Flora came to clear the tea things just as the twins were setting out. 'You shouldn't go out. It's going to be a wild night.'

'We're not going far. Just around the grounds, to give Monty a run.'

Flora still looked worried. 'Sir Ian wants us to live in until you go, but my daughter's not well again. The grandchildren are staying with us. My sister looks after them during the day, but she needs a hand at night — '

'I can't think why on earth Sir Ian

165

wants you to stay. We're all right — really. Why don't you both go back home?' Cressida zipped up her waterproof and pulled on her hood.

'Och, no! We'll do as Sir Ian wants. Ben'll run me back soon, stay a while, and then come back to Quoyne House to sleep. Don't you be long now, there's a mist coming down, and it's easy to get lost on Pentsay if you don't know the tracks.'

'We'll be fine. We shan't wander from the main track. Must give Imogen a last taste of good, clean, country air.'

Imogen looked doubtful and cast a longing glance at the fire, but loyally followed her sister. She'd enjoyed the morning thoroughly, but wasn't too sure about venturing out in the dark, swirling mist of the night. She was used to bright streets and pavements!

Her premonition was justified. It was dusk when they set out for what was intended to be a short walk, keeping the lights of Quoyne

House in view as a beacon. It was Montague who threw them off course. He ran away and was out of earshot in seconds. They followed, turned an unfamiliar corner, and Quoyne House disappeared. Backtracking, they called out for the dog, stopped and waited. Rapidly, dusk gave way to darkness, and the rain started again. There was an impenetrable fine curtain of misty drizzle.

'Where are we?' Imogen's voice was high. 'I can't see a thing.'

'Don't worry. I've got a flashlight. We're not far from the main track.' Cressida spoke with more confidence than she felt. She knew the area so well by daylight, but in the dark it was a different matter.

'We seem to have wandered off the main track — we're on some sort of a path,' Imogen said, a little fearfully.

Cressida's torch-beam cut through the mist, only to show thicker mist beyond. 'We'll just walk on for a while. We'll be certain to see Quoyne House soon. Where's that wretched dog? He probably knows the way back.'

'Don't you?'

'I think so. Anyway, it's impossible to get lost in Pentsay. It's too small. We have to hit the coast — or the village — '

'If we can find the track — '

More than an hour later, Cressida was feeling less sanguine, and Imogen was beginning to panic. Their progress seemed circular. They'd come back to the same stunted clump of trees twice and were no nearer finding the road.

'Cressy.' Imogen's voice was quavery, and she was shivering. 'I'm really soaked through. Will we have to spend the night out here?'

'Of course not. Look,' she exhaled with relief, 'here's the main track. We must be near the loch, too — down there — see that black glint. We must have walked miles in the wrong direction. Jon's boathouse can't be far. Cheer up, Imogen, he'll take us back to Quoyne House.' She took her sister's arm, and kept the flashlight shining downwards, so as not to lose the path again.

'I'm — scared, Cressy. I'm sorry but ...' Her voice rose to an anguished wail as she pointed to a tall shape looming out of the mist in front of them.

Cressida, startled, spun round jerking the flashlight upwards.

The tall figure bore down on them, and there was something in its upraised hand. She dropped the torch, grabbed Imogen's arm and, as fast as possible, ran from the menacing figure.

Then, out of the darkness, came the most welcome sound — the roar of a motor engine! Headlights wavered towards them, cutting through the mist and drizzle. She stood in the middle of the track, waving frantically. Imogen clutched her arm in terror.

'It's all right — it's Ben!'

Imogen gasped, 'Thank goodness,' as the Jeep stopped and Ben jumped down. Montague had been sitting alongside him, and if ever a dog could look anxious, he did.

'Where've you been,' Ben rasped. 'Flora's been scared half to death. She wouldn't go back to the village until you came back, and when Montague turned up — on his own . . . '

'Sorry. I lost my bearings.' Cressida bundled Imogen into the front seat.

'It was the Mountain Man,' Imogen stuttered through clenched teeth.

'The what?' Ben started the engine.

'Nothing,' Cressida intervened quickly. 'Just a tree — In the dark a bush becomes a bear . . . Come on, let's get back. Hot bath and soup, I think.'

Imogen perked up wonderfully under Flora's ministrations, and both girls sat by the fire, in dry clothes, sipping mugs of scalding, home-made soup.

Flora had blamed herself for letting them go out at all, and had refused to leave until she was assured that they were all right. Ben had practically forced her into the Jeep, promising the girls that he'd be back soon.

Cressida knew she was beaten. She dialled the airport on the mainland, before realising how late it was. The small local airport was closed — the last flight had left hours earlier. She dialled Heathrow. In answer to Imogen's raised eyebrows, she said tersely, 'I'm leaving Pentsay. I'll fly back with you tomorrow.' But, she'd been out of civilisation so long, she'd forgotten about seat booking problems — Imogen's flight was fully booked, and Sunday night was the first available one to London. She made a provisional reservation.

'But why?' Imogen asked. 'Tonight was just bad luck. I don't really think that was the Mountain Man.' She was sheepish.

'Nor was it Gordon Kinross,' Cressida answered grimly, 'but it was someone trying to scare us — someone who wants us out of Quoyne House.'

'But that's impossible Who could know we would be out on that track in the mist at that time of night?'

'Someone seizing an opportunity. Someone who'll go to any lengths to get us — me — out. We were almost at the boathouse. He could have seen us.'

'Cressy, that's ridiculous. You can't mean Jon. Why should he want you out of the way?'

'I don't know, or care any longer, but I can't stay now. It's just not worth it.'

'Jon Grant wouldn't do such a thing — and you can't believe he was the prowler the other night?'

'I don't know what to think any more. I know something strange is going on, and I don't particularly want to become involved. I shall miss Flora's soup.' She smiled. 'Don't look so worried, Imogen, you'll be out of here in the morning. Let's go and get some more soup.'

'OK. I'm not worried, just baffled.'

Flora had left the soup on the stove. It was still warm, but Cressida switched on the hob to re-heat it.

Imogen's frown deepened. 'But I don't see — ' Then she noticed Montague, who'd padded after them. He stood rigid, his neck hairs bristling, a low growl starting in his throat. Ears alert, nose turned in the direction of the cellar, he increased the growl volume.

'What now?' Cressida opened the door leading to the cellar. Montague bounded down the steps, barking loudly. She felt a sudden surge of fury. She was heartily sick of this silly game — she'd settle it once and for all. She picked up a heavy iron frying pan and headed for the cellar.

'Cressida,' Imogen shrieked.

'Stay there.' Cressida, adrenaline racing through her, ran after Montague. The cellar door was locked but, even through Monty's racket, she could hear sounds. She ran back and bumped into Imogen who was on her way down. 'Quickly — the keys — on the dresser.'

'Don't go in there, Cressy — '

'I'm not scared of Jon Grant — '

She seized the key-ring and flicked through the bunch. The key to the cellar door was the only big, old-fashioned one. She charged down the steps, unlocked the door, and flung it open. The long, low room was ablaze with light, but was deserted. Montague raced ahead, and Cressida took a few tentative steps inside. As she did so the lights went out and, seconds after, what sounded like a thousand bottles crashed to the floor.

She heard Imogen call out, 'Lights.'

Then there were more crashings and barkings. A door slammed — she heard Ben's voice above, and the lights came on again.

'Cressy, are you all right?' Imogen hurled herself down the steps.

Ben followed her, carrying an iron crow-bar. 'The lights fused. Is there anyone down there?'

'Not that I can see. Broken bottles. Ian's precious wine dripping from the racks — a lot of broken glass . . . Oooh . . . '

She gave a strangled gasp as Jon Grant slowly walked from the other end of the vault. He looked dazed as he put his hand to his neck, and Cressida saw there was blood on his forehead. It was at that moment of high drama, when she thought he'd been harmed that the suffocating knowledge swept over her — it was far more than physical attraction that she felt for him — she was in love with Jon Grant — whatever he was, or had done. Transfixed, she stared at him.

'Did you see them?' Ben said urgently.

'Only one of them. He lashed out at me, then ran off.'

'You're hurt. What's happened?' Cressida ran forward, dropping the frying pan with a clang.

Jon looked surprised to see her. 'It's nothing. You both have to leave now,' he said. 'I told Ian, but he wouldn't believe me. I know them.'

'I am going,' she whispered, staring into his grey eyes, wondering how she was going to be able to live in London without him.

Imogen was the practical one. 'You should see a doctor. That's a nasty cut. Probably needs a stitch.'

Jon looked annoyed, but blood was still flowing from his temple. 'Ben, you stay here. I'll go by Dr Fox's. I'll see you in the morning, Imogen. You, too, Cressida, if I have to carry you off Pentsay myself.'

'No. I can't get a flight until Sunday evening.'

'But you are going?'

'Yes.'

He closed his eyes briefly. 'At last,' he said.

9

'He might have been seriously hurt!' Imogen shuddered, and took a sip of Sir Ian's best malt. She'd convinced Cressida that she should join her — shock therapy — and had even persuaded Ben to take a dram, although, if she thought it would loosen his tongue, she was much mistaken.

It was Ben who had cleaned off the blood from Jon's forehead, confirmed the jagged cut, and phoned Dr Fox to warn him Jon was on his way.

'If Sir Ian, or Jon, want you to know anything, they'll tell you,' was his only answer to their persistent questions later.

'At least tell us how the intruders got in.' Cressida, although shocked by the night's adventures, was relieved and happy to know Jon wasn't responsible for trying to frighten her away. There was obviously a mysterious third party — or parties.

'The trap was baited,' was all Ben would say before he left to double-check the locks on doors and windows.

Cressida was mad with frustrated curiosity, as well as being in emotional turmoil, knowing that her heart was hopelessly committed to Jon Grant.

He arrived next morning to take Imogen to the ferry. Apart from a small, gauze dressing, he showed no ill effects from the night's mayhem and, he, too, maddeningly refused to talk about it, his main priority clearly was to get both girls to leave.

He spoke firmly to Cressida. 'You can stay over at Flora's, and I'll take you to the airport on Sunday. Wasn't last night enough? You're only complicating things by being here.'

Darkly attractive in the morning sun, his full, determined mouth drew Cressida's eyes. She felt shy, certain her feelings were blazoned across her face. She took refuse in sharpness. 'If you'll tell me what's going on, I might consider it. They weren't ordinary burglars last night were they?'

He scowled. 'I'll go this far. They mean business, and they'll be back. You're in the way, and it could be serious. Don't be such a fool — there's nothing to be gained by your staying at Quoyne House now. Why can't you trust me?'

'Cressy, he's right. I'll be worried sick if you don't leave. You're just being stubborn.'

'Well said, Imogen.' Jon was determined, and Cressida felt she had no choice.

She pushed her hair away from her face and looked directly at him. 'All right — you win. I'll pack now. Take Imogen to the plane. Ben'll run me to the village later.'

'I'll come back for you.' Relief chased away the scowl.

'Don't bother.' Cressida's heart was heavy. To leave Quoyne House, and not to see him again!

'No bother. I want to make sure you go,' he said grimly, as he slung Imogen's bags in the Land-Rover.

Cressida waited until they were out of sight before turning sadly indoors. There was a terrible sense of anti-climax. The mystery of Quoyne House was unsolved, and Jon Grant would remain for ever an enigma.

A horrid thought struck her — maybe she'd have to tolerate him as a brother-in-law. He seemed very taken with Imogen, who made no bones about being attracted to him, although, with her, it was automatic to respond favourably to every attractive male. Cressida permitted herself the luxury of a final, heavy sigh, then went briskly into action to take her mind off things.

It didn't take her long to pack. Ian had taken the folk-lore books she wanted, promising to send them round to her London flat. Her clothes and files of material were soon bundled together, and it was still barely mid-day.

Montague followed her around even more closely, clearly sensing that something was amiss. Her heart was wrenched. She knelt down and fondled his silky ears. He whined softly and nuzzled her cheek. 'I'm going to miss you so much,' she whispered, 'but you'd hate London — the traffic, the noise — no rabbits, no fields.'

The brown eyes spoke volumes, he nudged her face again, and she abruptly changed her mind. 'All right then — I'll come back for you. Maybe you would like it — Highgate Woods — the Heath — ' It was an alluring prospect. She'd give it a try. The world looked momentarily more cheerful, but time still hung heavy after she'd taken Montague for a last walk.

She made a final tour of the house and grounds before making herself coffee. Flora was in the village. Saturday was her day off, and Ben was around somewhere. She called him for coffee; his answering call came from the direction of the cellar, and she went to find him. The door was open, and he was clearing up the broken glass and spilt wine. She looked around with interest — it was the first time she'd seen the wines properly, and her godfather had an amazing collection. Racks of dusty bottles stretched along one wall, and huge wooden casks were piled up against the other. 'Are they full of wine?' she asked incredulously.

'Och, no! They used to be for whisky, when the distillery was working. They're just decorative now.'

'There's some amazing stuff here.' Cressida very carefully picked up a dusty bottle. 'This one's absolutely priceless!'

'Careful!'

Ben, usually so phlegmatic, looked so agitated that Cressida couldn't help laughing. 'There — it's safely back. Sir Ian told me he has a case of 1966 Lafitte for me in here. Do you know where it is?'

'I do.' Ben answered with great

reluctance. 'You can look,' he added grudgingly.

Ben led her to the centre of the vault, where a number of smaller tunnels converged. 'The 1966's are down here.'

He'd indicated a cavernous area, but Cressida stopped. 'Ben, there's a draught, from over there. I can feel the fresh air. Is that the other exit — into the grounds?' Lafitte forgotten, she moved swiftly to follow the air current. It was quite some way along, at the end there was an open door leading to another short tunnel which ended abruptly at a heavier door, also ajar. She was about to push it open, but Ben was too quick for her, he darted ahead and slammed it shut.

'Is this how they got in last night? Come on, Ben, you've got to tell me.'

He frowned. 'I can't tell you. Leave it, please.'

'There was no other way to get in,' she said defiantly, and then remembered Ben's frantic gardening efforts, and the bonfire. 'It was deliberate. You cleared that entrance.' She recalled Ben's enigmatic words — 'the trap was baited'. 'They, the prowlers, are to be lured here for what? You aren't telling me anything, Ben — I'm just guessing out loud. They were obviously looking for something valuable. But why would you leave valuables here — at risk? And what's Jon Grant got to do with it? Or Sir Ian? All right, Ben, I won't worry you any more — show me the Lafitte, and then we'll have coffee.'

Ben's relief was great as he led her to the precious bottles stored in their rectangular, wooden cases.

She touched the one marked Chateau Lafitte, 1966. 'You're as old as I am.'

'I'll take this broken glass up. I'll be back to close up.' Ben said.

Cressida nodded, still absorbed, then, ran her hands along the boxes with their famous names. What was that one? It was slightly out of line with its fellows. She pushed it back, and slid it too far. Now it really was out of line. It seemed very light to contain a dozen bottles. She pulled it forward, and sprang back as it toppled towards her.

Horrified, she watched it bounce to the ground, and breathed a sigh of relief when it remained intact. She stooped to lift it back up on to the pile of wooden boxes. The top was loose, and she could slip her fingers under the lid. The wood came away in her hands and, with a gasp, she saw, not twelve bottles of fine wine, but bundles of currency. Gingerly, she picked one up — it was a wad of £10 notes, and the box was full of them.

Wide-eyed, but cautious, she knelt and lifted out several layers. The bundles did not reach the bottom of the box, but were resting on papers which, to her not very practised eyes, looked like securities or bonds. There was a fortune stashed away in that case of 1966 Latour! She sat back on her heels. This must be what all the fuss was about. But whose was it? And did Jon know about it? Why leave it there?

Ben called down, 'Cressida, are you all right?'

She opened her mouth to call him down, to show him what she'd found — then closed it. She needed time to think. Sir Ian should be told — after all, it was his cellar. 'Coming.' She hastily tidied up the bundles, rammed the lid on, and pushed the wooden crate underneath a rack. There was no time to stow it properly — already, Ben's footsteps were on the stairs. She sprang up, ran to switch off the lights, and slammed the door to. 'Coffee Ben? I'm dying of thirst. Don't worry. I've locked up, and switched off the lights.'

10

The coffee was calming, although Ben seemed even more jumpy than Cressida. After a few attempts at polite interest in his grandchildren, she gave up and took her coffee into the library.

After some hesitation, she phoned Sir Ian. His secretary told her that he was in Brussels, at a conference and could only be contacted in an emergency. Cressida decided to try again later.

Restlessly, she paced around Quoyne House. The uncertain weather had turned stormy again, as the clouds rolled in, promising a downpour sooner or later. By mid-afternoon it was already quite dark.

She was relieved to see Ben out in the grounds. If Jon didn't come for her, at least Ben could take her to Flora's. A flash of lightning made her blink, but the rumble of thunder was still far off. She saw Ben hurry indoors, and felt very isolated.

Upstairs, she had a final check round the bedroom. After its spacious luxury, the flat was going to feel cramped for a while. Carrying her case on to the landing, she ran straight into the picture of the Laird Kinross, just as another flash of lightning lit up his glittering stare. She nearly dropped her case, before quickly running downstairs.

'This is getting spooky,' she muttered to herself. She thought of the wooden wine box in the cellar — it was an awesome burden, and she longed to shelve its responsibility. She tried to contact Sir Ian again but he was still unavailable. The storm came closer, and lightning flashes were more frequent. She was in a dilemma — she could drive herself to Flora's, or get Ben to take her, but that would leave Quoyne House with its secret unrevealed and unguarded. She must wait until Jon came.

It was almost dark before he came. Montague's joyful bark sent her running into the hall, and into Jon's arms. She was so relieved to see him, she didn't question the use of his own set of keys to Quoyne House.

'Cressida! Sorry I'm so late. Would you believe the Land-Rover got stuck in a ditch!' He looked extremely fierce and forbidding. 'Are you ready? There's not much time. I want you away from here.' He'd his arms around her when she'd run into the hall, but now he held her away from him and his expression changed to one of concern. 'What is it? You're not scared of the storm, surely?'

She shook her head, and all the words came tumbling out. 'In the cellar . . . the 1966 Chateau Latour. There are thousands of pounds . . . and papers. I found it by accident, and didn't know what to do — I phoned Ian but — '

Jon grabbed her shoulders and gave her a little shake. 'Calm down, Cressida.

When did you find this? Does Ben know?'

'No. He was clearing up the broken glass . . . and there's another entrance.'

He gripped her so tightly, she cried out, and he relaxed his hold. 'Show me quickly — and then you must go.'

'Why? You must tell me what's happening.'

'There's no time. This storm — it'll give ideal cover. I've sent Ben for help. I've been tracking the yacht. I should have insisted you left Quoyne House earlier. If anything happens — ' He caught her hand, and led her towards the cellar. 'I'll shut Montague in the library. I don't want him scaring them off.'

'Scaring who off? Who are they?'

They reached the cellar door, and Jon went to unlock it. 'They,' he said bitterly, 'are the pair who bankrupted my business, and robbed my life of five hundred and four days.' He switched the lights on. 'Where is it?'

'Over there, but how . . . ?'

Jon went over and knelt by the box, pulled it out, and lifted the lid. 'This is it! What I've been looking for for weeks — and you stumble upon it by accident. It's incredible!'

A vivid flash, and an almighty crack directly above, made Cressida jump. The lights dimmed and flickered — she heard a muttered oath, and felt herself alone in the fading light. For a few moments, nothing happened, and the storm thundered on overhead.

She felt her way forward. 'Jon? I can't see very well.'

'Hold on. There's a flashlight by the door. The storm's affecting the generator.'

A match flared, and Cressida saw Jon's face deeply shadowed, before he moved away. She heard him stumble, saw the match drop, and then fear flooded through her as she saw a chink of bright light at the garden end of the cellar. The door slowly began to open, and powerful flashlights swept across the vault, cutting swathes of brilliant light in the darkness, and throwing huge shadows on the walls. She instinctively drew back, and at the same time felt her arm gripped, and Jon's whispered voice in her ear.

'Keep absolutely still. They're here — at last!' He pulled her away to clasp her even more tightly against him in the dark corner behind the stack of 1966 crates.

The flashlight beam came nearer, and Cressida held her breath. Shafts of light criss-crossed the cellar walls. Voices were clearly audible. 'Blast this storm — I can't remember exactly — it's so dim in here.'

Cressida felt Jon stiffen, and a small sound in his throat made her clutch his hand.

His answering squeeze reassured her, as a woman's voice said, 'I can remember perfectly. If you'd have let me come down last night, we'd have it safely on board now, and be miles away. And,' she said sharply, 'I shouldn't have been such a fool as to tackle Jonah Cameron.'

'That was an accident. I didn't realise it was him. I thought it would be safer if it was just me — '

An impatient voice interrupted him. 'Here — this is where it should be.' The voice was only feet away from Cressida's ear. The torch light bobbed upwards. 'It's not there. That's where we left it — I know we did.'

'Don't panic. It's here — on the floor.'

'How?'

'Shut up. Just put it all in the bag. Hurry.'

'It shouldn't be on the floor. The lid's off, Harry, something's wrong.'

Cressida could see a dark shape kneeling by the crate, stuffing notes and papers into a bag. Another figure stooped over him, directing the beam of light.

Jon Grant leaped forward and knocked the kneeling figure to the ground. Cressida heard two screams, her own, and that of the woman.

The flashlight was knocked over, but she saw the two men grappling on the ground, the woman picking up the bag and making for the entrance. Cressida moved to follow her, but tripped over the writhing figures, and fell. She thought she must have knocked herself out into some sort of nightmare hell, as both cellar doors burst wide open, and powerful lights illuminated the scene in stark black and white relief. She saw Ben, with a uniformed police officer and another man, move into the cellar, trapping the woman with the bag.

Jon yelled, 'Ben — here. I've got him. Where's Cressida?'

'Here,' she gasped out, practically underneath the flailing feet.

She saw Jon thrust the man towards the policeman, before he stooped and swiftly gathered her in his arms. 'Cressida! Are you all right? You're not hurt?' His hands caressed her face, touched her lips. She shivered as his arms tightened around her. Whatever was happening was worth it! She savoured the brief moments in his arms. 'Ben — emergency generator. The storm's affecting the main power. The police are in control. We need more light!'

★ ★ ★

'I need some explanations.' Cressida said.

Ben had fully restored the power. The two policemen had eventually taken away the man and woman who'd broken into the cellar, and the contents of the Latour crate were securely locked in Sir Ian's safe. Ben had gone back to the village, and Jon was to follow with Cressida.

'I do owe you an explanation — and an apology.' Jon's voice was quiet.

'Apology?'

'First, for taking you initially to be a spoiled media star. No, let me go on. I'll answer as many questions as you like, but hear me out first.'

'Go on then,' she prompted. 'Who

were the man and woman in the cellar?'

'Harry and Estelle Bowman.' Jon seemed pleased to have a direct question as a starting peg. 'They are — or were — my partners in Cameron Enterprises, and they were responsible for its collapse and — and for my abduction and captivity. They set me up, and like a trusting fool, I fell into their trap. There was nothing political about my incarceration, but they timed it to appear so. They're very clever operators.' He smiled ruefully. 'That's why I originally chose them to be partners in the firm.

'You've surely read about political hostages. The Bowmans paid handsomely to have me treated in the same way, but that worked in my favour in the end — because I was lumped in with the politics, I was part of the negotiating deal. I don't suppose I'll ever know the full story, but I was released early — about six months before Estelle and Harry had expected. They'd paid for a two year sentence.' His mouth tightened, and Cressida put her hand in his.

'It must have been awful,' she said simply.

'It was. Life will never be quite the same again, just as,' he touched her scar, tracing his finger down its length, and this time she didn't flinch, 'it will never be the same for you. We should understand each other, Cressida. We both have scars.'

'I know, but you can live with them. I'm learning to live with mine. Why did your partners do this?'

'The oldest motive in the world. Greed. Money. A long-term two year plan to milk Cameron Enterprises dry, and transfer its assets abroad to their personal bank accounts. After two years, just before I returned, they planned to disappear, leaving me to face the creditors on my own.'

'But why Quoyne House. I don't see — '

'They were using Quoyne House

as a holding post, before transferring currency abroad. After each fraudulent transaction, they waited, ready to transfer the funds back to Cameron Enterprises if the auditors were suspicious. Apparently they weren't. I'm afraid, in my absence, it was all too easy — that's why I had to be removed. Sir Ian is a good friend of Cameron Enterprises, and he often invited the three of us to his house parties, so Estelle and Harry got to know the place pretty well, and had duplicate keys cut.'

Cressida shuddered. 'So they did break in? They'd been inside the house when Imogen arrived?'

Jon nodded. 'Presumably — but each time something went wrong — the cellar door was jammed, or Monty raised the alarm. And I startled Harry the other night.'

'How did you know they'd be here?'

'Your godfather and I have been working with the Fraud Division of the Metropolitan Police. You see, Harry and Estelle were at a Quoyne

House party when news of my release came through. It coincided with one of their cash transfers. They'd liquified a sizeable chunk of Cameron Enterprises' assets, ready for later deposit in foreign banks. My guess is that they panicked, hid the cash in the cellar, couldn't get back to it — and had to run before I arrived in England. As you know, it wasn't long before I found out what had been going on.'

'How did you know about Quoyne House?' she said shakily.

'Thanks to Sir Ian. He's a most astute man, with a sixth sense for trouble. He was suspicious of Estelle and Harry all along, and overheard a whisper of conversation. He put two and two together, followed a hunch, and persuaded the Fraud Squad to let me escape and hide up here. He found out that they had chartered a yacht in Spain and were sailing north. Ian was convinced they were coming back to pick up the last of the money they'd embezzled. I'd been searching for it when you arrived.'

'So it was a trap. That's why Ben cleared the garden entrance?'

'We sensed they were getting desperate. Tonight was their fifth attempt. We reckoned they wouldn't risk the front door again. Harry had made a solo attempt last night, and found the entrance. When they set out from Spain, they assumed Quoyne House would be still shut up for the winter, and they could simply walk in and pick up the money. But that's enough story telling. It's all over, and I can get on with my life.'

Sadness flooded Cressida's soul, There was a lot more she wanted to know but managed to keep her voice light. 'Back to London?'

'I don't know — yet. There's a lot to clear up at Cameron Enterprises, but — it depends on you, Cressida.'

'Me? Why me?'

Jon took her hands and pulled her up to him. 'Because, it can't have escaped your notice that I find you attractive, and — because I find the idea of a future without you, impossibly bleak. From that first moment, when you flung yourself at me like some demented fury, you've invaded my heart and soul.'

'But you were so — angry — so — '

Jon bent and kissed her, and from then on Cressida was lost in a sweet tide of sensation which carried her beyond all questions. There was silence for a long time as they savoured the blissful recognition of mutual love.

When he spoke, his voice was soft with passion. 'I had to clear up this business first. You were beginning to obsess me, and I had to remain single-minded until Harry and Estelle were caught. We were so close, I couldn't let go. There was so much at stake. I had to try to put you out of my head — but now, at last, I can say it — I love you, Cressida. I want to marry you.'

Cressida touched her cheek. 'Doesn't this matter?'

He kissed her so thoroughly, she had little breath left to argue! Then he answered. 'You are, Cressida. With or without — even because of that scar. That's how I first knew you — that's what I love — all of you. But, if it bothers you, we'll go to Edinburgh, see James Stewart, the cosmetic surgeon — '

This time, Cressida interrupted him, standing on tiptoe to slide her arms round his neck, swinging her hair away from her face as she did so. 'No,' she whispered. 'Maybe one day, but here and now it doesn't bother me at all. Wherever your fate is, so mine will be. Always and for ever. I love you, and I'll joyfully marry you.'

They were in the hall, Jon holding Cressida closely to him as though he would cleave her to him for eternity. At the front door he stopped and threw a set of keys on the table. 'I shan't need these again. I have everything I'll ever want right here.' He stooped and kissed her, then opened the massive front door. On the threshold, Cressida turned for a last look at the Pentsay Lairds guarding the staircase. It had to be her imagination, but they looked so much more kindly and benign — and she half expected them to nod approval as she and Jon, closely followed by Montague, went out of Quoyne House to begin their shining future together.

THE END

We do hope that you have enjoyed reading this large print book.

Did you know that all of our titles are available for purchase?

We publish a wide range of high quality large print books including:
Romances, Mysteries, Classics, General Fiction, Non Fiction and Westerns.

Special interest titles available in large print are:
The Little Oxford Dictionary Music Book, Song Book Hymn Book, Service Book

Also available from us courtesy of Oxford University Press:
Young Readers' Dictionary (large print edition) Young Readers' Thesaurus (large print edition)

For further information or a free brochure, please contact us at:
Ulverscroft Large Print Books Ltd., The Green, Bradgate Road, Anstey, Leicester, LE7 7FU, England.
Tel: (00 44) **0116 236 4325**
Fax: (00 44) **0116 234 0205**

VOYAGE INTO PERIL

Shirley Allen

Julia had spent the past three years in America with her mother and stepfather, George. After the death of her mother, Julia decided to return with George to the Isle of Man, where she had been born and brought up. As they sailed from New York on board the Lusitania, she met again the man who had stolen her heart years before. But danger lurked in the seas. Was the love she longed for to elude her yet again?

THE FLAUNTING MOON

Catherine Darby

Purity Makin is only a girl when James Rodale, a handsome cavalier, seeks shelter at Ladymoon Manor, the house on the moors which holds strange echoes of its sinister past. But the girl has the passions of a woman, and from the events of a night springs a tale of promises betrayed and twisted jealousies; a tale in which a sacred chalice is used for good or evil to satisfy the desires of those who discover the secret of the Moon Goddess.

A MAN FOR ALWAYS

Nancy John

After the plane crash that robbed her of her memory, they told her that her name was Jayne Stewart, and she could only accept and tremble. She trembled with humiliation, for Jayne was cold and calculating, a woman who hadn't cared when her husband died. And she trembled with passion, passion for her husband's brother, Duncan, a man who had sworn to hate her. What was the truth about her past? Would she find it in time to bring her love in the present — and for always?

DANGEROUS LOVE

Caroline Joyce

Rebellion had brought many hardships to her beloved country and Rosaleen feared for the safety of her father and brothers when they became involved in the 1798 County Wexford rebellion. When she meets Captain Geraint Glendower, the brother-in-law of the farmer for whom she works, Rosaleen finds herself becoming very attracted to him. But the last thing she needs in these troubled times is to become torn between her family and her love for a British army officer.

SHADOWS OF THE PAST

Margaret McDonagh

To take her mind off her Great Aunt Rosemary's pending operation, Holly decided to visit Pagham Harbour Nature Reserve. When she became stuck in the mudflats, handsome Rick Cunningham came to her rescue. Holly found herself becoming attracted to Rick, who was a partner in a firm of architects in Chichester. But when he told her of his plans for Rosemary's cottage, she was shattered. How could she ever trust him again?

PENDRAGON:
THE WIZARD'S DAUGHTER

Katrina Wright

In the winter of 1594, Nimue, daughter of the Queen's 'other Welsh wizard', has left London for North Wales to find her destiny. The playwright Will Shakespeare follows her as his Dark Lady, but she has met Merlin Pendragon, the scarred lord of Pendragon tower, and feels they have shared a passionate bond in the past. Against the background of land-greed and fever for the newly-discovered Welsh gold, Nimue and Pendragon are married. But before she can go to him, events overtake them . . .